W9-AHV-286

Walkin' on Clouds

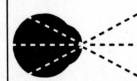

This Large Print Book carries the Seal of Approval of N.A.V.H.

AN ANGELS & OUTLAWS
HISTORICAL ROMANCE, BOOK 2

Walkin' on Clouds

Carolyn Brown

THORNDIKE PRESS
A part of Gale, Cengage Learning

Detroit • New York • San Francisco • New Haven, Conn • Waterville, Maine • London

GALE
CENGAGE Learning®

Copyright © 2011 by Carolyn Brown.
An Angel & Outlaws Historical Romance Series #2.
Thorndike Press, a part of Gale, Cengage Learning.

LIBRARY OF CONGRESS CATALOGING-IN-PUBLICATION DATA

Brown, Carolyn, 1948–
    Walkin' on clouds / by Carolyn Brown.
        p. cm. — (Thorndike Press large print clean reads) (An angel & outlaws historical romance series ; 2)
    ISBN-13: 978-1-4104-4248-2 (hardcover)
    ISBN-10: 1-4104-4248-9 (hardcover)
        1. Sisters—Fiction. 2. Kidnapping—Fiction. 3. Louisiana—Fiction. 4. Texas—Fiction. 5. Large type books. I. Title. II. Title: Walking on clouds.
    PS3552.R685275W35 2011b
    813'.54—dc22   2011033335

Published in 2011 by arrangement with Thomas Bouregy & Co., Inc.

To my wonderful editor,
Lia Brown,
with much appreciation!

CHAPTER ONE

Fairlee Lavalle awoke from the worst night-mare she'd ever had to find she had not been dreaming. Her ordeal did not end when she opened her eyes, no matter how many times she blinked. The damp, moldy smell filling her nostrils wasn't a figment of an overactive imagination, and the constant swaying was very real.

She was really belowdecks on a ship, lying on a cot so narrow that one hand had fallen to the floor and gone to sleep. There was really a storm with thunder rattling the rough wood walls around her and lightning so bright that its glow lit up the high window in the small room where she was, apparently, being held prisoner. Every time the ship rolled, so did Fairlee's stomach. She had no idea how she'd gotten there, how long she'd been asleep, or who the man was sitting on a chair in a corner with his chin touching his chest.

She was absolutely sure that she hadn't gotten onto a boat voluntarily and that the man was not her fiancé, Matthew Cheval. The rest was a foggy blur. She wiggled her toes. Shoes were on her feet. Her arm across her stomach weighed as much as a whole ham, but she forced it up enough to see that she was wearing the same thing she'd had on when she went up to bed the night before. But wait. Had it been the night before, or longer? How many days had she worn the long-sleeved blue cotton dress with a sprig of green leaves scattered in the design? She drew her dark eyebrows down into a frown and tried to remember if she and Matthew had said their wedding vows before she was snatched. Nothing materialized.

Dear Lord, she'd been kidnapped on the eve of the most important day of her life! Her eyes were heavy, but she refused to blink for fear she'd fall back to sleep. She had to stay awake. She had to get back to the plantation in time for her wedding. She wasn't a weak woman. She'd been taught to hunt, ride, and shoot. Her guard was foolish if he thought she wouldn't do him in with his own gun. Give her half a chance, and he'd be bleeding on the wood floor.

No one kidnapped a Lavalle and got away

with it. She'd show him that he'd have been better off dragging a hungry Louisiana alligator down into the dingy cabin than Fairlee Lavalle. When the cobwebs left her mind, the devil himself wouldn't be strong enough to contain her on that boat, so the guard had best get himself rested up, because he was about to wake up to a full-fledged war.

You are now officially a tainted woman, her conscience chided.

It's not my fault, she argued. *Matthew will understand.*

He almost didn't before, and this is twice as bad, the argument went on.

She set her jaw and refused to think about it.

It wasn't her fault that she'd been snatched right out of the plantation house at Oak View; it was a kidnapping. She wasn't alone with a strange man of her own accord. Nothing untoward had happened. She was fully dressed and even had her shoes on. He hadn't hurt her or compromised her.

That ugly, niggling little voice of her conscience reminded her that Matthew had already made sly remarks about how she should appreciate his gesture in proposing, since not many men would have after that

9

trip last spring. That hadn't been her fault either. She hadn't even wanted to go to Texas, but her sisters had talked her into it. She sure hadn't wanted to pretend to be a nun for a week or to travel back to Louisiana with three outlaws. Oh, sure, they'd been perfect gentlemen the whole journey, but Matthew kept saying little things about how there was talk that more had gone on out there in the Texas wilderness than just escorting the Lavalle sisters home to Oak View. She'd assured him so many times that she'd lost count that absolutely nothing had happened other than that her sister, Delia, had fallen in love with Tyrell Fannin.

"I'll explain," she whispered to herself with a weak smile.

She and Matthew would stand before the preacher and say their vows as soon as she made her way back to the plantation. Nothing was going to stop her. If this was a kidnapping for ransom, Matthew would send the money immediately.

He never has said that he loves you, has he? So what makes you think he'll send money for a woman who has spent at least one night in the company of a man? He won't marry you after this, and you know it.

"He's going to tell me he loves me on our wedding day when we share our first kiss," she tried to argue, but her mouth was too dry to get out anything more than a raspy mutter.

Her trunks were packed to move from Oak View to his plantation home, and her beautiful lace wedding dress hung in the massive oak wardrobe, waiting for her to wear it tomorrow . . . or was it yesterday? She couldn't remember, but it didn't matter. There would be rejoicing when she got home, and Fanny would put the sugar icing on the cake. It would be a beautiful wedding full of memories to last a lifetime.

Matthew would tell her how beautiful she was and how much he loved her after the wedding — she was sure of it. And he was right; after that trip with three outlaws she and her sisters were all tainted. Delia had gotten off easy when she married the oldest of the outlaws and went home with him to Greenville, Mississippi.

Men didn't come dashing out from every bush in north Louisiana, making offers for Fairlee or Tempest's hand in marriage, when they found out that they'd spent weeks in the company of disreputable outlaws. But then, they hadn't done so before either. The Lavalle women had a reputation for being more than a little independent and willful. Uncle Jonathan often said it would take a strong man to win the hand of any of his nieces, especially the youngest one, Tempest.

Fairlee frowned. Where was Tempie? Had she been taken too? No, she didn't think so. She remembered that Tempest had gone down to New Orleans to spend a few weeks with their cousins, and suddenly Matthew had begun to ride over from his plantation frequently to seek out Fairlee's company. Aunt Rachel wasn't happy about it, and Uncle Jonathan warned her that the man was in debt and could possibly be interested only in her dowry. It wasn't hard to fall in love with Matthew, though. He was dashing, with his dark hair and handsome-beyond-description looks, even if he did insist that they wait until their wedding day to kiss her or say the three words that she wanted so badly to hear.

Tyrell told Delia that he loved her when he proposed, and I know he kissed her on the trip from Texas, her mean conscience continued to nag.

She ignored it and slowly scanned the tiny room. The small cot took up more than half the space. The door was closed and bolted from the inside. Her trunk was shoved up next to the bed. Why would a kidnapper bring along her things? That made no sense at all. She jumped when the man in the chair snored even louder than the next clap of thunder. She pushed back Aunt Rachel's quilt and squinted at him. He was dressed in such common clothing. Matthew would never be caught in rough-spun trousers and a worn wool coat. But he looked vaguely familiar. If he'd just raise his head, she was sure she would recognize him.

Everything in the small quarters began to spin when she sat up, so she fell back on the cot and pulled the covers to her neck. What should she do? If she eased out the door and ran, there would be no place to go except overboard. She'd freeze to death before she made it to shore in the cold December water. She was too dizzy to attempt the takeover of a ship with nothing more than a quilt to use for a weapon. She had no idea how long she'd been knocked out or where she'd land or if it was possible she could swim to a shoreline.

Isaac Burnet roused when he heard a sound, but when he looked over at Fairlee, she was sleeping. She must've moaned and adjusted her position, as she'd done several times in the past few hours, making enough commotion to wake him. He tucked his chin back down to his chest but couldn't get back to sleep. If he ever got off this rocking boat, he

13

swore he'd never get on another one. He wasn't cut out to be a sailor; he liked good, solid ground under his two feet. Not even for his cousin's wife — Fairlee's sister, Delia Lavalle Fannin — would he have consented to ride down the river in a boat that rocked back and forth with every gust of cold north wind. Had he known he was going to have to kidnap Fairlee and then take her away on a ship, he'd have refused Delia's request to summon and escort her sister to Greenville, even if it did make her cry.

He had had absolutely no doubt that Fairlee was going to be a handful when he set out on the trip, and he had not been disappointed. When he delivered the letter from Delia, Fairlee would have dropped him graveyard dead if looks could kill. When she finished reading it, she told him that he could go back to Mississippi, that she would not call off her wedding the next day.

That's when her younger sister, Tempest, came up with the abduction idea. Aunt Rachel and Uncle Jonathan joined in the plan, and by bedtime everything was in place. Then, it had seemed like the only way to save Fairlee from a big mistake. Now, he wasn't so sure. Shooting her in the leg so she couldn't stand up to marry the money-grubbing idiot might have been a better choice. Putting up with her sass all the way to Mississippi would have him yanking out his hair or hers.

He looked over at her resting on the cot. She looked so peaceful, with her dark lashes resting on her perfect face. But looks could be deceiving. Just like they'd been last spring, when he and his brother and cousin thought they were bringing three nuns out of Texas. Turned out to be three hellcats named Lavalle who wore men's britches and could outride and outshoot most men on the face of the earth.

He hoped they were off the water and in the stagecoach before Fairlee came to her senses. He'd seen his fair share of her temper when he and his brother, Micah, along with their older cousin, Tyrell Fannin, escorted the three sisters from the Alamo to Bennet's Bluff, Louisiana. Any one of the Lavalle women could scorch the hair off Lucifer's horns with a glare from her blue eyes. They'd all said that Tempest had the quickest temper, but he'd always thought Fairlee had the sharpest tongue. No doubt about it, when she woke up, she'd use it like a machete to cut him to pieces.

Back in the spring he and his brother, Micah, along with their cousin, Tyrell, had traveled all the way to central Texas, chasing the man who'd murdered their father for his horse. They'd found him a day too late. The fool had been killed in a cantina brawl the night before and cheated them out of sending him on a personal visit to Lucifer.

It was near dark when they arrived in San Antonio and got the news that the lowlife had been killed. They'd planned to head back east the next morning and had gone into a cantina for a drink before they found a hotel room. They'd been minding their own business when a Mexican man accused Tyrell of flirting with his woman, and that's when the fight had started. Truth of the matter was that they'd ridden for weeks in search of the murderer and wanted to fight *something,* so it only took a few harsh words before Tyrell popped his accuser in the jaw. When the smoke cleared, there were more wounded Mexicans than Mississippi men, so they were the ones who ended up in the San Antonio jailhouse.

Just when they thought they were going to go plumb stir-crazy, Captain Robert Lavalle had offered to bail them out and pay them handsomely to take three Sisters to Bennet's Bluff, Louisiana. The story was that he wanted them to be out of harm's way when the fighting at the Alamo began.

They'd been on the road a week when they found out the ladies weren't nuns at all. They were sisters of the blood, not Sisters of the faith, and Captain Robert Lavalle was their father.

Isaac rolled his neck to get the kinks out and looked his fill of Fairlee. To his way of thinking, she'd always been the prettiest one of the sisters. Tyrell would argue about that, since he and Delia fell in love and married at the end of the trip, and he thought he got an angel when he married her. And Micah might argue that Tempest was the prettiest, with her curly dark hair and smoky eyes, but not Isaac. Still, as much as Isaac respected Delia, he'd never put an *angel* tag on any Lavalle. Especially not Fairlee.

He remembered the morning they'd first seen the women in the wagon. They'd been dressed like nuns, but something wasn't right even then. They laughed too much, and their eyes were always full of mischief. A week later he was shocked when they appeared in men's pants, but he wasn't completely surprised that they weren't really nuns.

His mind went back to the trip and all the things that had happened. They'd found a burned-out homestead along the way, the man and the woman who lived there murdered. Only a baby remained, and Fairlee had taken it under her wing like a momma hen with a chick. Her bright blue eyes had gone all soft, and she'd agonized over giving that little girl to the warmhearted settlers they'd met later.

"Well, her eyes dang sure ain't goin' to be all sweetness and honey when she finds out that she's been kidnapped on the eve of her wedding day," he whispered to himself.

That big dose of laudanum that her Aunt Rachel and her sister Tempest had dosed her evening tea with wouldn't last much longer. Isaac inhaled deeply and tried to get himself ready for a hissy fit. He just hoped the boat could withstand the stomping Fairlee Lavalle would do when she figured out she wasn't getting married, she was going to Mississippi, and it was Isaac Burnet who would be escorting her. Someone once said that hell had no fury like a woman scorned. Well, it could easily be reworded to say that hell was a picnic compared to a Lavalle who didn't get her way.

"I wish you would've been able to come with me, Delia," Isaac mumbled.

Delia was the whole reason he'd made the trip from Greenville, Mississippi, to Louisiana. She'd sent several letters to Fairlee when she found out that her sister was going to marry that rascal Matthew Cheval, but she'd gotten no response. Time was drawing near for the December wedding, and Delia asked Isaac to hand-deliver a letter to Fairlee. She was too far gone with the baby to go herself, and she was terrified that Isaac wouldn't get there in time to stop a disastrous wedding. He'd ridden twenty hours a day and arrived half dead on his feet to find that the wedding was to be the next day at midmorning.

Aunt Rachel was wringing her hands, Uncle Jonathan was cussing mad, and Tempest was about to explode. The three of them came up with the abduction plan, and he'd reluctantly agreed. There was nothing else they could do, and he'd made a promise to Delia that he would bring Fairlee back to Mississippi. So they'd dosed her up and bought tickets on a ship down to St. Charles.

He'd tried to reason with Fairlee, had given her the letter. She'd read it and then tossed it aside without so much as a second glance. That's when he would have liked to shoot the woman. He hadn't promised Delia he'd bring her back alive, and Fairlee was more stubborn than Tyrell's old plow mule.

Isaac had thought they'd travel by horseback or stagecoach, but Jonathan had assured him that that would be too slow if Matthew made a show of trying to chase them down.

The thing to do was go south by river until the next day, and when the boat stopped in St. Charles, they could hire a stagecoach to take them back north toward the Arkansas border. Thank goodness no one in Greenville would have to know the particulars of how they'd gotten from Bennet's Bluff across the top of Louisiana, through Arkansas, and into Mississippi. Fairlee's reputation would be better in Mississippi than it had been in Louisiana anyway. And after she stopped ranting and raving and pouting, she'd see that Delia and Tempest had both done the right thing.

Eventually, she would see that Matthew Cheval was only after the Lavalle sisters' money and that he didn't care which one he had to stand up with in front of the preacher and vow to love until death parted them to get the cash. Crazy fool man. There wasn't enough money in the whole world to make Isaac marry a Lavalle woman. Tyrell had gotten the best of the lot when he married Delia. The other two, Tempest and Fairlee, should've been left at the Alamo.

Looking back, Issac figured that if they

had left the younger Lavalle sisters at the Alamo with a gun for one and a knife for the other, the Texas soldiers could have packed a picnic and taken it out into the green pastures; when Santa Anna arrived, the Lavalle sisters would have whipped El Presidente and his whole army, who would have scooted on across the border with their tails tucked between their legs and howling as if the devil himself was chasing them. Santa Anna wouldn't have even wanted Texas if he'd had to go through the Lavalle sisters to get it. And it would have saved Sam Houston so much trouble.

Fairlee opened her blue eyes wide and gasped. She swallowed twice before she could speak. "What are *you* doing here, Isaac Burnet? You're supposed to be on your way back to Mississippi."

Isaac got ready for the first round and wished they had put the whole bottle of sleeping medicine into her evening tea. Tempest should have realized it would take more than two doses to keep a wildcat asleep for any length of time. Come to think of it, they could have sent what was left in the bottle with him, so he could keep her drugged at least halfway to Mississippi. He sighed and hoped that the ship they were on could stand up under a storm on the outside and a mad Lavalle on the inside. That much pressure from both sides might blow them all to kingdom come. Saint Peter would take one look at Fairlee, double lock the pearly gates, and hide behind a cloud. Even then she'd probably kick down the gates and go after him.

"I asked you a question. Answer me!" Her speech was still slightly slurred.

"What am I doing? I'm sitting here watching you, wishing I was anywhere else in the whole world. When the boat docks, we will get into a stagecoach and go north as far as it will take us, then we'll travel like we did from the Alamo to Bennet's Bluff — on horseback. *You* are going to your sister Delia's house, Fairlee. I told you when I arrived at the plantation that you were going with me one way or the other. This is the other," he said coldly.

"I will not! You take me back home right now. I'm getting married tomorrow morning at ten o'clock." She sat up and grabbed her aching head. She blinked several times before the room stopped spinning and he was back in focus. "Delia put you up to this, didn't she? She can get married and have children, but I'm not supposed to do the same."

"Well, I dang sure wouldn't have kidnapped you for any other reason. If you think I'd take you because I wanted to, then you've got rocks for brains," he said.

"Turn this boat around, and take me home."

"Can't. Besides, it's too late. You didn't make it to your wedding, and the note Tempest gave Matthew Cheval says that you are sorry to cause him so much pain and hurt but you figured out at the last minute that you loved me and we've eloped. It says that when I came back and proposed, you realized I was the only man for you. Kind of like Tyrell was the man for Delia. It's all a big pack of lies, thank God, but Tempest had a swell time writing the note. Matthew is already crying into his expensive whiskey because he's still broke and the likeliest Lavalle sister was too smart to fall for his wicked charm. He could never hoodwink Delia or Tempest like he did you," Isaac told her bluntly.

"That's hateful!"

"That's the truth. Cheval is a wicked man who was only marrying you for your money," Isaac argued.

"I love him," she said between clenched teeth.

"No, you don't. You might love the idea of love. You just want to be married and settled

23

so folks won't call you an old maid."

She jutted her chin out. "I do love him."

"When you're walkin' on clouds as high as you were, you could see fluffy wings and a halo on the devil himself. You don't love that man, and he dang sure doesn't love you. In a month you'd both be miserable, and Delia knew it," Isaac said.

"He'll understand if I go back home and tell him Delia was behind this. He knows how devious my sister can be." She threw herself back on the cot. It smelled like old, worn-out wool socks. The walls surrounding her were rough enough that if she ran her fingers across them, she'd bring back a handful of splinters. When she inhaled, she could smell whiskey and tobacco.

The boat listed to the right, and she hung on to Aunt Rachel's double-wedding-ring quilt, but it didn't keep her from landing flat on the floor. When her bottom thudded against the planks, Isaac Burnet chuckled, and she shot him a drop-dead-on-the-spot look.

"Aren't you going to be a gentleman and help me up?" she asked. When he extended his hand, she'd pull him down and smother him with the quilt. Danged man anyway. She'd told him that she wasn't going to Mississippi, that she was going to marry

Matthew, and that there was nothing he could do about it. He hadn't listened worth an owl's hoot and deserved to die by having the air squashed from him.

"You are a Lavalle. You've been taught to ride and shoot like a man, and you've proved it. You don't like me, and you've told me that so many times, I couldn't count them. I don't like you well enough to care what you think about me. I'm tired, so no, I'm not going to be a gentleman. Stand up on your own," he said.

It wasn't that Isaac wouldn't help her, but he was afraid that if he put out his hand to do so, she'd do something crazy like throw him across the room, take his rifle, and shoot him with it. Besides, he really didn't care if Fairlee thought he was a rascal. He'd promised to take her to Delia. He hadn't promised to mollycoddle her on the way.

"You, sir, are a cad," she hissed, at the same time that a mouse ran across her lap on its way to its hole on the far side of the room.

She jumped up and did a little jig in the small space between the bed and the door.

He chuckled. "I thought you Lavalle women could take on a grizzly bear bare-handed."

"Don't you dare laugh at me! I hate mice

and spiders."

"That's funny. I figured you'd grab Lucifer by the horns if he ever crossed you." Isaac chuckled.

A loud clap of thunder made Fairlee grab her ears and forget the mouse. "I've died and gone to hell," she moaned.

Isaac grinned even bigger. "I expect you feel like that right now. I danged sure do when I think of all those miles I've got to put up with your smart mouth. But I bet in a year you'll be thanking Delia for saving your silly hide. It will take me a lot longer to forgive her for sending me to keep you from your folly."

She sat down on the cot and kept a watch on the mouse hole. "When does this thing dock? You don't have to take me back home. I'll find my own transportation."

"Haven't you listened to a single thing I've said, woman? If you went back now, you'd be a tainted woman. You left a note that you were eloping with me. In Greenville, no one will know about the note, so you'll be fine there, but in Louisiana you are now a marked woman — even worse than you were before," he said.

"I can make it right," she whispered.

But she couldn't. The trip from the Alamo back to Louisiana in the company of three outlaws had stained her reputation. Matthew might overlook a stain; he wouldn't abide a full-fledged mud bath.

She jutted out her chin. "And don't you call me *woman!*"

Isaac slowly shook his head. "You think you can make it right, then you are still walkin' on clouds. Drop on down here to earth, and shake that craziness out of your head. You'll realize you ain't got but one choice, and that's to go to Delia's with me. When we get there, you can bet I'll stay on my side of the plantation. I'm here to tell you, I durn sure don't want a Lavalle, so you ain't got a thing to worry about either on the trip or after it's done. And what should I call you? *Man?*"

"By my name. Just plain old Fairlee or maybe Miss Lavalle."

"Humph," he snorted.

She pulled her feet up onto the cot and wrapped her skirt firmly around her ankles so the mouse couldn't climb up under it. Isaac was right about her ruined reputation, but she didn't have to agree or even nod at the man. He was every bit as full of himself as he'd been on the previous trip.

Why did this have to happen to her? She was the one who didn't want another adventure. She was the sister who wanted to settle down to a nice, quiet lifestyle on the Cheval plantation and raise a couple of children. Now she'd be an old maid for sure, because her name would be in shambles after she'd traveled all over the countryside with a man.

"You going to pout?" he asked.

"I do not 'pout.' " Each word was more definite than the last — and louder.

"Well, what do you call what you're doing, then?" he asked.

"I'm thinking."

He shook a finger at her. "If you're contemplatin' a way to escape, you might as well forget it, Fairlee. I promised Delia I'd bring you to Mississippi, and that's where you're going. It's up to you whether you go hog-tied over a horse's back or riding the critter. To be honest, I'd just as soon hog-tie you."

She pointed back at him. "Don't you point that finger at me, and you aren't big enough or strong enough to tie me up at any time. You are a fool if you think you are. I'll let you know when this thing docks what I'm going to do about this situation you've gotten me into. How long was I asleep anyway?"

He shrugged. "More than twenty-four hours. We got on this boat at midnight. Way I figure, it's about midnight now, so you should've gotten married about fourteen hours ago. By the time we dock, it'll be a whole day since you were going to make the biggest mistake of your life," Isaac said.

They'd really been on the ship only about six hours. Even so, she wouldn't have time to race back home and throw that fancy lace dress on before Matthew Cheval arrived, but making her think she'd lost a whole day might convince her to go with him to Mississippi peaceably instead of finagling a way to escape, run back home, and get her pretty little neck into more trouble than both of them could get her out of.

She turned her back to him and stared at the wall. "You are an abominable man. I shall never forgive you."

Isaac grinned. "I don't really need your forgiveness to keep on living, Fairlee. But I couldn't have managed this on my own. Delia, Tempest, your Aunt Rachel, and your Uncle Jonathan all helped out. You're the only one with your head in the clouds. Everyone else knows that Matthew Cheval is lower'n a snake's belly. So, are you ever going to forgive them?"

"Matthew is not that low, and my sisters wouldn't do such a stupid thing. You did this all on your own," she insisted.

The fog in her brain began to evaporate,

and she remembered Aunt Rachel telling her to drink all her tea.

"Tomorrow is an important day," she'd said with a smile.

Tempest had poured her another cup and sat on the edge of the bed while she drank it, kissed her on the forehead as she fell asleep, and shut the door.

Fairlee remembered drifting into an odd sleep that she figured was brought on by the excitement of becoming a new bride the next day. She'd thought she was dreaming that someone carried her over the threshold and that Aunt Rachel said to wrap her favorite quilt around her because it was cold out. Looking back, it hadn't been a dream at all but what had really happened. Isaac Burnet had carried her outside, and they'd wrapped a quilt around her because it really was cold.

"It wasn't a dream after all," she mumbled.

"What did you say?" Isaac asked. He wasn't worried about her trying to run until they were on firm ground. She wasn't stupid, except when it came to men. Besides, the storm wasn't letting up. It sounded as if the rain had turned to sleet as it beat down upon the deck overhead.

"*You* carried me out of the house, and

Tempie put something in my tea," she said.

Just wait until she got ahold of Delia and Tempie. They were in for a fight like they'd never seen before. She didn't meddle in their lives and decisions, and they had no right to get into the middle of hers.

"Yes, I did. And put you into Jonathan's carriage and took you to the dock, where we boarded the ship. Jonathan knows the man who owns this old tub, and we paid him well for you to be comfortable. The bad weather started right after we got into the cabin," he explained.

She waved her hands around to take in the whole room. " 'Cabin'? This isn't anything but a closet."

"It happens to be the captain's cabin, and it cost us twice as much as the only other one on board. If I'd known you were going to act like this, we'd have stayed topside under a slicker. Your sister insisted you have the best," he said.

"Well, bless Tempie's little heart. Maybe I won't yank *all* her hair out when I see her again," Fairlee said.

"Can I watch? I'll put my money on Tempest. I think she could take you in a fight. She's pretty vicious," Isaac said.

Fairlee spun around and glared at him. "Tempie flares up quickly, but the fire goes out just as quickly. I stay mad a long, long time, so you'd better watch out. I'll get even when you least expect it."

Isaac, Fairlee reflected, was the most handsome of the three outlaws who'd escorted them home from Texas. He had thick, dark brown hair combed straight back. In the sunlight it had chestnut highlights. If she believed in such things, she'd think that his mossy green eyes held magical powers, because when he looked at her, little shivers danced up her backbone.

She'd never tell him, though, and she'd never forgive him for ruining her life.

CHAPTER TWO

Fairlee sat with her back against the rough wood wall and dozed. She came fully awake when someone knocked heavily on the door and shouted, "We're here, Mr. Burnet. We came to haul the trunk topside. Your journey is over, but the rain is still coming down, so button up your coat, and put your hat on."

Isaac wished it *was* over, but in reality his journey had barely begun. In two weeks, when he handed Fairlee over to Delia, his trip would be finished. He vowed that when it was, he was going home and not even visiting Tyrell and Delia until the baby came.

Fairlee pushed the quilt back, stood up, and shivered. She grabbed the cover and wrapped it around her like a shawl. "Where are we?"

Isaac stretched and unlocked the door. "St. Charles. We unload here. We'll have time to stop at a local inn for food, and then we'll catch the stagecoach north."

"It took us a day and a half to get to here?" She frowned.

"Bad weather prevented them from loading the cargo," he said.

She groaned. "Matthew would have rescued me if he'd known."

"He might have rescued your money. He wouldn't care what happened to you," Isaac said.

"You have to be the meanest person alive," she snapped.

"Maybe so, but I'm also the most honest," he smarted off right back at her.

"I've decided to go to Delia's. There seems to be no alternative, since you have made sure my good name is in the chamber pot," she said.

Isaac's eyes widened. "You are supposed to be a lady, and they don't talk about chamber pots in front of men."

"I can be just as honest as you can, Isaac Burnet, and that's exactly where you and my sisters have put my reputation, so why shouldn't I say it aloud?"

The argument ended when someone rapped on the door again. Isaac threw it open to find two burly sailors. They wore heavy wool coats that had seen better days and knee-high boots with their trousers tucked into the tops.

"We thought you didn't hear us," the bigger one said.

"Tempie packed your cape. I'm supposed to tell you that," Isaac told Fairlee.

Fairlee threw open the clasps and opened her trunk. Her winter cape was right on top, and she hugged it to her face like a long-lost sister. Made of dark brown wool, it had an oversized hood and was lined with rabbit fur.

"You going to wear that thing or carry it like a baby?" the smaller sailor asked.

"Don't you worry about what I do with it." Fairlee swung the cape around her shoulders, looping the long ties into a bow under her chin. She folded the quilt and put it into the trunk before closing the lid.

"Ready?" Isaac asked.

"As I'll ever be. But there *will* be a reckoning." Her tone dripped icicles.

"Whew! I'm glad you got to travel with her, not me," the bigger sailor said.

Isaac stepped back to let the men get a handle on the trunk. "I'd rather it was you. I already put up with her on one trip across country. It ain't easy, and I'm not looking forward to the rest of this one."

"I'm right here," she said coldly.

Isaac nodded. "Yep, you are, and we agreed to be honest."

35

"Well, truth be told, it wasn't a piece of cake traveling across country with you either," she said.

The shorter sailor sighed. "She sounds just like my wife. Her sharp tongue is what put me to work on a ship."

The bigger one held up his palms. "That's what set me to work on the water too. Wife is always glad to see me when I come home for a couple of days. I'm always ready to leave when they're done. I wouldn't go on a trip with my wife or yours for no amount of money. Why'd you marry yours, if you knew she was hard to get along with?" the bigger one asked.

"We are not . . ." Fairlee started to protest.

Isaac touched her arm and shook his head. "Love is blind as a bat and crazy as a courtyard fool, ain't it?"

"You got that right. We'll go on up topside, and you can follow us," the big man said.

"Marry in a hurry, and you get a whole lifetime to regret it," the smaller fellow told them when he set the trunk on the dock beside a stagecoach.

"You, sir, should be a poet," Fairlee said.

"So, you are admitting that you were about to make a mistake in marrying that worthless Cheval?" Isaac asked.

She clamped her mouth shut.

The shorter sailor chuckled. "Saved her from a bad mistake, did you? Well, here's hoping she gets sweeter. Good day to you both. Stage leaves in an hour. It'll take you up to the first stop for two dollars and a fence rail each or else two and a quarter each without a fence rail. There's an inn that serves a pretty fine breakfast about a five-minute walk to the north. Good luck, man. I got a feelin' you're goin' to need it."

He disappeared into the foggy mist and left Isaac and Fairlee standing beside her trunk. She looked around at the desolate dock and the cold gray morning and wanted to throw herself to the ground and pitch a little-girl fit. She was supposed to wake up at the Cheval plantation this morning, a new bride ready to make her husband happy, not to a wet dock that smelled like raw fish and rats.

She threw back a side of her cape and shook a finger at Isaac. "Don't be thinking I'll get any sweeter with the passing of time. It's going to take until the spring thaw for me to be civil to my sisters, and you've got a long way to go past that. And why would the stage charge more if you don't have a fence rail?" She frowned.

"I'd figured on a year or two at the least

to melt your icy nature. I don't care if you're ever civil to me. I hope we don't see each other often enough for it to matter. The fence rail is to help get the stage out of the ruts if it gets stuck in bad weather like we're having right now. I didn't bring one, so we'll have to pay more," he told her.

"Easy, boy," a deep voice said, as a man sweet-talked a horse from the boat's deck onto the dock. "One more step and you'll be on steady ground."

Isaac made a clucking sound, and the horse settled right down and let the man lead him to its master.

The man laughed as he handed the reins to Isaac. "Too bad that don't work with your woman."

"It took a while to train the horse. I expect it'll take even longer to get a woman into shape," Isaac said.

"Prob'ly so," the man agreed with a nod.

Fairlee stomped her foot so hard on the wooden dock that it sounded like thunder. "You will never 'train' me."

The man stopped and looked over his shoulder.

Isaac shrugged. "Maybe never will get the job done."

The man laughed and disappeared into the fog.

Fairlee stared at the beautiful black animal. "You going to ride that thing or let it sit on your lap in the stagecoach?"

"Don't be hateful. He'll be tied to the back of the coach. When we reach the end of the line, then I'll ride him."

Anger filled Fairlee from her smallest toenail to the top of her head. "Don't you talk to me about being hateful. I've every right to be any way I want to be. You and my relatives betrayed me."

Isaac shook his head. "We betrayed no one. We thwarted Cheval's wicked plans and saved you from a life of misery."

She refused to answer or argue.

"Ready?" Isaac asked.

"You talking to me or the horse?" Fairlee asked.

Isaac set his jaw and glared at her. "The horse is always ready. He doesn't talk back, and even when he's hungry, he's got a better disposition than you do."

"Ready for what?" Fairlee asked.

"It's going to be a very long ride in that stage. We need to eat and buy food for the day," he said.

"I'm hungry, if that answers your question, and I expect I'll be hungry later on in the day as well."

A man appeared from the front of the

stage. "Y'all ridin' with us today? Horse going too? I'll buy the critter from you if it's for sale."

"I'd sell this woman first," Isaac said.

Fairlee shot him a killing look. "And I'd shoot you between the eyes if you tried."

The man shook his head. "No, thank you. I'd buy the horse, but I like my women a little softer-spoken."

"Some days I can't get a break." Isaac grinned. "Come on, woman, let's go find some breakfast. Stage don't wait for nobody, not even you."

Fairlee slapped the air beside his arm. "I told you not to call me *woman*. I can ride as well as you and shoot better. And you'd best stop insulting me, or I'll prove both. Then you can explain to Delia why you're coming home empty-handed."

The driver's laughter rang out into the foggy morning.

"Don't make brags that you can't back up with actions," Isaac said.

She set her jaw firmly. "I'm not boasting. I'm stating facts. Go find us some breakfast and see if you can buy a loaf of bread and some cheese for later in the day. I'm not leaving my things for any hooligan to steal." She promptly sat down on top of her trunk.

"Anybody tries to steal anything off this

stage, I get to shoot 'im." A big red-haired Irishman poked his head around the other side of the coach. " 'Tis my job to watch out for thieves and robbers, ma'am. I'll be ropin' your little trunk there on top of the stagecoach while you're gone. Just don't be late gettin' back, or else it'll be gone north, and you'll be sittin' right here without it," he said.

She stood up slowly and nodded.

Without another word, Isaac and the horse started walking toward the inn.

Fairlee would be hung by a worn-out rope if she tagged along behind him like the horse. She hurried to catch up and kept in step right beside him, which wasn't easy, since his stride was so much longer than hers.

Why would Tempie and Delia interfere with her life anyway? Poor Matthew was probably despondent and worried and getting no help from any of her family. She wondered what Fanny had done with the cake she'd baked, then scolded herself for worrying about something so silly.

I'll never get to wear my beautiful wedding dress now. It was Mother's and fit me so well, and it was supposed to bring me good luck in my marriage. Did *it bring me luck? Was I not supposed to marry Matthew? Were Delia and*

Tempest right? If they were, then Isaac is right too. Drat it all, I can't think straight anymore. I need food and time to figure all this out.

Warmth rushed out to greet them when Isaac opened the door into the inn's dining room for Fairlee. The horse made a noise at the hitching post, as if telling them that it wasn't fair that they could go inside where it was warm and he had to stay outside in the cold mist.

She dropped the hood of the cape when she was inside the door, and six people turned to stare at her. When Isaac followed her in, the customers went back to eating. He had no doubt that they would all remember Fairlee, with her looks and the way she carried herself like royalty. If Matthew Cheval did come looking for her, it wouldn't be long until he had plenty of people telling him that she'd passed through the inn. With any luck, the man would lick his wounds and then go shopping for another rich bride, but Isaac couldn't trust in that. And he had a sudden desire to put miles and miles between him and Louisiana.

A large woman with a white apron covering her dress motioned them to a table near the blazing fireplace. "Sit right here," she said. "Do you need a room? We've got two available for the day and night."

"No, just breakfast. We have to be on the stagecoach within the hour. Could you prepare some bread and cheese for the day's journey?" Isaac asked.

She nodded. "I have a nice smoked ham we're slicing for breakfast. With this weather there's not many who are stopping. Would you like me to wrap some of the ham?"

"That would be wonderful." Fairlee shrugged out of her cape, letting it fall across the back of her chair. The blaze in the fireplace crackled as it devoured the logs and chased any chill from the room. She should have been looking at the fireplace in her bedroom at the Cheval plantation that morning. Matthew would be propped up beside her, telling her that he was the luckiest man in the world to have her for a bride, and he'd kiss her ever so sweetly.

"You walkin' on clouds again?" Isaac asked.

She spun her head around so quickly that it made her dizzy. Crimson that had nothing to do with the heat from the fire crept into her cheeks. Surely Isaac Burnet could not have read her thoughts.

"She was thinkin' about something more important than clouds." The woman winked. "I'll get that food right out. Young married couple like y'all needs to keep well for yer honeymoon."

"Thank you," Isaac said.

The woman disappeared into a back room, and Fairlee stole covert glances at the other patrons. They dined on slabs of ham, eggs, and biscuits. Her stomach growled loudly, and she laid a hand on it.

"Hungry?" Isaac asked.

Either you are getting slow, or else the drugs aren't out of your system yet, Fairlee's nagging inner voice said. *You just let Isaac pretend you were newlyweds, and you didn't even put up a fight about it.* Her gaze went to Isaac's face.

"I'm *very* hungry. I haven't had a bite of food in more than twenty-four hours. Why did you let that woman think we're married?" she whispered.

"If Mr. Cheval comes looking for you, he'll be looking for a kidnapped lady, not a bride sitting sweetly at the table with her new husband. Don't worry about your good name, Fairlee. These people will never see us again. And most likely they'll never lay eyes on Cheval. He doesn't really love you, Fairlee. He tried to get Delia to marry him, and when she said no and married Tyrell, he just moved on down the list." Isaac spoke softly.

Fairlee's dark eyebrows knit together in a

44

deep frown. "Yes, he does. A man doesn't ask a woman to marry him if he doesn't love her, and I love him enough for both of us anyway."

"Like I said before, you are walkin' on clouds. And that's a stupid thing to say anyway. There ain't that much love in the world. If you really knew Cheval, you'd realize he won't ever be a giver. He'd take and take and take from you until you were nothing but a shell with no heart or soul left."

She took a deep breath and let it out slowly so she wouldn't make a scene right there in a public place. "You don't know that, Isaac Burnet. You were only in his company one evening. Besides, what makes you think he would never really fall for me? Is there something so terribly wrong with me?"

"A man should be proud to have you for his wife. There's nothing wrong with you but your bad judgment. And, Fairlee, one evening tells a man a lot about another man. He looked at you Lavalle sisters with dollar signs, not love, in his eyes," he said.

The innkeeper returned to set a plate of food before each of them. "Coffee or tea?"

"Coffee, black," Fairlee said.

Isaac nodded. "The same."

The woman smiled. "Good food will stop your arguing."

"Let's hope so." Isaac smiled back.

"It almost always does. Can't quarrel while you're eatin'." The woman headed back to the kitchen.

"It'll take more than food to put a stop to your rude opinions," Fairlee said.

"And yours," Isaac retorted.

Fairlee decided to let him have the last word. She was hungry, and they had a long ride ahead of them. If they missed the stage, it might be hours, even a whole day, before they could catch another one. And now that she'd resigned herself to go to Delia's, she was anxious to be on her way. She'd have at least two weeks to get a speech ready to scorch her sister's ears for having her kidnapped, and she was eager to work on that.

They ate in tense silence.

Fairlee had no choice, really. A decent woman didn't go to a ship's captain and ask for passage alone back up the river to Bennet's Bluff. Nor did she ride that far through the wild countryside without an escort, even if she could take care of herself. Actually, she reflected, Tempie had set this whole thing into motion when she'd sided with Isaac, Delia, Aunt Rachel, and Uncle Jonathan, and dosed Fairlee's tea. She'd known that she was leaving Fairlee with no options, and for that she was due a rousing good fight also.

Fanny used to tell them when they were little girls that they had to own up to their deeds. Uncle Jonathan called it accepting responsibility for their actions. Well, Tempest Lavalle and Delia Lavalle Fannin had a reckoning on the way, so they'd best clean off a spot right smack in the middle of the living room floor, because Fairlee would need lots of room for the fit she was going to pitch. And her two sisters could accept the responsibility for their actions and take her tongue-lashing.

Things were coming back to Fairlee in bits and pieces. She remembered being carried outside into the cold night with a quilt wrapped around her and Tempie saying, "Tell Delia I'll be there before that baby is born, and that's a promise."

Well, come right on, little sister. I'll get you both with one big fight, Fairlee thought, as she finished the last bite of ham and biscuit.

Isaac polished off the last of his breakfast and motioned for the innkeeper. She brought the food she'd prepared for the journey and laid it on the table between them.

"How much do we owe you?" he asked.

"All total, I reckon a dollar will cover it," she said.

He pulled coins from his pocket. "How far is it to the next stage stop?"

"About twenty miles. It's a hard day. My cousin and his wife have a stop there. Only got two rooms upstairs for the guests, and she's not as good a cook as I've got in the kitchen, but they're honest people. She'll fix you up with vittles for the next leg of your trip. Where are you going?"

"Monroe," Isaac said.

"Live there?" she asked.

"Not yet, but we might if we like it," Isaac said.

"Well, you'll be a good five days getting up to Monroe. Me and my husband come from that area ten years ago. Ain't been back, but I hear it's growed up a lot since then. Good day to you."

"Thank you." Fairlee pushed back her chair and pulled her cape up over her shoulders. She tied the strings under her chin and flipped the hood over her head.

The woman studied Fairlee for a moment, pocketed the money, and went on to the next table. "You're welcome," she threw over her shoulder.

"She looked at me strangely," Fairlee said,

as she and Isaac stepped out onto the porch and the icy wind hit them.

"Not you. That cape. Lots of women would give their right arm and half their children to have something like that. Where'd you get it anyway?" He untied the horse and led it back toward the stage.

"All three of us sisters have one. The wool was grown on the plantation. Delia is quicker with a knife than Tempie and I are, so I'll have to give her credit for most of the rabbit skins lining the capes. Tempest designed them, but we all had a hand in the actual sewing."

"How come you didn't have them on the trip from the Alamo?"

"We didn't take them. Texas was supposed to be hot enough that we would never need them."

"Stage leaves in five minutes!" the driver yelled from the topside seat.

Two women, one elderly and one quite young, hurried from the opposite direction, arriving at the same time Isaac and Fairlee did. The driver crawled down the side of the coach and held out his hand.

"That'll be two and a quarter dollars for each of you to the first stop. Ten dollars each if you're going all the way to Monroe," he said.

The young woman handed him four dollars and fifty cents. "Just to the first stop, please."

He looked at Isaac.

"We'll pay for today. Four dollars fifty, then?"

"Got a fence rail?"

Isaac shook his head.

"Then that's the price. I knock off a little for every able-bodied man willin' to help me and Shooter dig the coach out of ruts, if he brings his own fence rail," the driver said.

"I didn't bring one, but if we get into a bind, I'll be glad to do my part," Isaac said.

"Thank you, son. I'm Cap, and the man who rides shotgun for me is Shooter. Not many bandits or Indians mess with him, big as he is. Reckon y'all met him before. He said a young married couple had gone to find food and left a trunk that he loaded up top."

"We did meet him," Isaac said. "I'll be tying my horse to the back. I hope that's all right."

"Looks like a fine animal that won't have no trouble keepin' up. Don't allow no mules or donkeys tied up, but I ain't got a problem with that horse right there," Cap said.

Isaac handed him four dollars and fifty cents, and he pushed an apparatus with two wooden steps up to the door. The windows were leather covered in an attempt to keep the cold out, but it would find its way in around the edges, Isaac figured. The elderly lady sighed and hiked her dress enough to keep from tripping as she bent her head and eased into the coach. She had a full face with two extra chins and enough girth that the cold wind would have a hard time reaching her bones to chill them.

Her young companion went next. She was of medium height and thin as a rail, had two teeth that were slightly bucked out over her lower ones, and sported freckles across her nose. They were settling into the bench toward the front of the coach when Fairlee got inside. Isaac followed quickly, sat beside Fairlee, and had barely gotten his bearings in the semi-darkness when the door shut.

The coach took off with a jerk. Both ladies across from him grunted, and Fairlee grabbed the edges of her cape and wrapped it tightly around her as if the rabbit fur and wool would keep her from tumbling onto the floor, or else being thrown across the short distance to land in the big lady's lap.

The driver yelled for them to hang on; there were ruts up ahead.

"Felt like we started off in a rut," the older woman grumbled.

51

"It's all right, Grandma. Hang on to the valise, and we'll be fine," the younger one said.

The young woman set a satchel between them, and the older one leaned on it like an armrest. Now there was no way another passenger would fit on that side if the stage picked up another customer. That meant if someone joined them, they'd have to sit beside Isaac, which would put him so close to Fairlee that he'd be melted into her side the whole day. He'd rather be hugged up next to the devil himself than Fairlee Lavalle. Come to think of it, there wasn't much difference between the two. The devil wasn't as pretty, but then, he wasn't nearly as hateful and mean, so it was a toss-up.

And I suppose you'd be as sweet as sugar frosting if someone stole you away from your wedding day. You'd be falling down on the ground, kissing the dirt at the toes of the woman who drugged you, carried you into a stinking room on a boat, and now was about to lead you on a two-week journey through the countryside, Isaac's conscience chided.

Isaac ignored the niggling voice and gave silent thanks that neither the stage driver nor the innkeeper had mentioned that it was Saturday. Fairlee hadn't questioned him when he'd said that it was already Sunday.

There still must be a residue of the drugs in her system, or she'd be asking why the inn was open for business on a Sunday morning. Thank goodness she hadn't, and they were on their way. The farther away from Bennet's Bluff they were before she realized that she hadn't lost a whole day, the better for Isaac.

If she'd known that she could have caught a different stage from St. Charles back to Bennet's Bluff that morning, she might have tried to get back in time for that wedding. Then Delia would have been furious with Isaac, and he'd have failed in his mission. Each passing mile they traveled toward Monroe made his job easier.

"So, you ladies are only going to the next stop?" he asked.

The older lady's head bobbed up and down, making all her chins quiver. "Yes, sir, we are. I'm Matilda Greenly, and this is my granddaughter, Polly. My daughter runs the stage station at the first stop. That would be Polly's mother. We're going to visit for a few weeks."

"I live with Grandmother and help her," Polly explained in a sweet southern voice so soft that Fairlee had to strain to understand her above the rattle of the coach wheels.

"Where are you going? Y'all been married

long?" Matilda asked.

"Only a few days. We're on our way home to Mississippi. I'm Isaac Burnet, and this is Fairlee," Isaac said.

Matilda's crystal-clear blue eyes twinkled in a bed of wrinkles. "Imagine that. Coming all the way down to Louisiana for a bride. It's going to be a long trip. Entertain us with the story of how you met."

Isaac chuckled.

Polly clapped her hands gleefully. "It must be good, Grandmother — a couple who lived so far apart. You are from Louisiana, aren't you?" she asked Fairlee.

"Yes, I am, but we met in Texas," Fairlee said.

Polly's squeal was high-pitched. "Oh, I can't wait to hear the story. Now I'm glad we decided to travel today instead of waiting until the first of the week."

Isaac looked at Fairlee. She gave no sign that she'd picked up on the fact that the day wasn't Sunday.

"Well?" Matilda was impatient.

Isaac cleared his throat and began. "A year ago a bandit killed my father in Greenville, Mississippi. Evidently he liked my father's horse and murdered him for it, because that's the only thing he took. My brother, my cousin, and I trailed him for weeks from

Mississippi to Arkansas, down through Louisiana and into Texas. We got to San Antonio the day after he'd been killed himself, so it was all in vain except that we got my father's horse back."

He paused.

"Now you tell why you were in Texas of all places, and in San Antonio. Were you there during that Alamo defeat?" Matilda asked Fairlee.

"My father was Captain Robert Lavalle. He was stationed at the Alamo. There are three of us daughters: Delia, me, and Tempest, born in that order. We went to the Alamo after our mother died to be a comfort to our father. Then the trouble came, and he wanted us out of harm's way, only there were no stages leaving or arriving. We three girls were trained to hunt and ride, so we could have taken ourselves home to Louisiana, but Father would have none of that. We even offered to stay and help defend the Alamo, but he wouldn't have that either. So he went to the jail and talked three outlaws into escorting us back home, since they would be heading in the same direction when they were set free," Fairlee said.

"How did you get into jail if you already had your father's horse and were eager to get back home?" Matilda asked Isaac.

"Don't leave out details, young man. I hate this trip. I wouldn't even go if I hadn't promised Polly when her grandfather died that I'd see to it she got to go home twice a year if she would come and help me. So entertain an old woman and tell me what happened next."

Isaac sighed. This was not the way he'd planned this journey. He'd figured he'd sit on one side of the coach with Fairlee on the other, shooting daggers at him from those cold blue eyes.

"There were three of us also: Tyrell Fannin, my cousin, and Micah, my brother. We only meant to get a drink in the cantina, but this Mexican fellow there accused Tyrell of looking at his woman wrong. Lookin' back, we were all itchin' for a fight. We'd been tensed up for weeks, trying to catch my father's killer, and been cheated out of giving him a good whippin' before we took him to the sheriff. So when the Mexican got all fired up and throwed the first punch, we were almighty glad to oblige him. When the smoke settled, he and his cronies looked worse than us, so the sheriff hauled my brother, my cousin, and me off to jail. We'd only been in that little cell a couple of days, but it seemed like eternity. When Captain Lavalle came and said he'd get us out if we took three Sisters to safety in Louisiana, we agreed. We would have captured Santa Anna for him if he'd asked us to do that to get out of jail. So we figured taking three nuns to safety wasn't any chore."

Matilda's brow wrinkled in more furrows than her chins. "Wait a minute! Are you a nun? Young lady, did you give up your calling to marry this man?"

Fairlee smiled for the first time since she awoke. "No, ma'am. My father didn't ever say that we were nuns. But when he said he had three sisters who needed to get out of San Antonio and back to Louisiana, these outlaws thought he meant Sisters of the faith. It sounded like a good idea to him. He figured it would be a wonderful way to get us past Santa Anna's army. So he located three habits, and even though we protested that God would probably strike us dead, he insisted that we were going to be nuns. We had to promise him that we'd wear the habits for a week. After that we were free to either leave them on for the duration of the journey or take them off and ride our horses, rather than sit in the back of a stupid old wagon."

"Well, I do declare," Matilda said. "Did you see that Santa Anna devil?"

"Yes, we did, and my sister even had to

say a prayer for him before he'd let us go through his army. You don't want to know what she told us she'd prayed." Fairlee giggled.

"So for a whole week you pretended to be nuns?" Matilda asked.

"Yes, ma'am," Fairlee said.

"And what did you three men do when you figured out the sisters weren't nuns?" Polly asked.

Isaac picked up the story. " 'Do'? We were madder'n wet hens after a spring rain. They all went up to their hotel room in them black and white things and came down the next morning in men's trousers and shirts, ready to ride astride horses instead of sidesaddle like women."

Polly clapped a hand to each cheek. "Oh, my! Did you really?"

Fairlee crossed her arms over her chest underneath the cape. "Our father taught us to ride and shoot like boys. Boys don't wear skirts when they ride, so we didn't either. We proved ourselves on the trail. We rode as hard as the men did, and we took care of ourselves from then on."

"What about when Tempie fell into the hole?" Isaac challenged.

"What hole? Oh, this is the best trip ever. Tell us about your sister falling into the hole, please." Polly's eyes glittered.

"We'd been traveling for many days, and when we finally stopped, Tempest and I went to . . ." She paused. "We went for a walk, and some wicked men had dug traps in the ground and then covered them with branches and grass so you couldn't see them, and Tempie stepped on one of them. The twigs beneath the grass gave way, and she fell to the bottom of a deep hole that had a skeleton in it — the remains of someone who hadn't been as lucky as she was."

"A skeleton!" Polly echoed with a shudder. "She must have nearly died of fright! Was she badly injured?"

"No," Fairlee responded. "She only hurt her ankle a little bit, but she was plenty scared. But even if Isaac and his fellow outlaws hadn't been there, we would have figured a way to get her out."

"Did you see the wicked trappers?" Polly asked, still shivering with delicious horror.

"No, and it took us hours to get out of the area," Fairlee went on. "Tyrell went first, poking the ground with a stick, before we could take each step."

"Did he find any more traps?" Matilda asked.

"Oh, yes, and we uncovered them all.

59

Hopefully, we foiled the trappers' chances to hurt and rob other folks, at least for a few days," Fairlee said.

"What an adventure," Polly sighed.

Fairlee shot a look at Isaac. "I'd hoped it would be my only one."

He shrugged and grinned.

"Do go on. What happened next?"

"Tell them about the baby," Isaac said. He liked the sound of Fairlee's voice in the darkness, and talking did help pass the time. Had Matilda and Polly not boarded the coach with them, the day would have worn on with no end in sight, tension building with every mile. Maybe telling the stories would make Fairlee less angry at him for kidnapping her.

Fairlee remembered the infant clearly and poignantly. When they'd first gotten back to the plantation, the baby had come to her mind often. But with the wedding preparations and the notion of a child of her own to come someday, she'd tried to forget her memories of that little girl.

"We came upon a farm that had been raided. It looked like Indians at first glance, but later we learned that it could have been murdering white men posing as Indians. The couple who lived there had been killed, and the mother had fallen shielding her baby, who was still alive. It was a little girl, and my sister Tempest really watched over her the most. We all took turns holding her until we came to another farmhouse. A couple who couldn't have children lived there, and the woman fell in love with the baby. It was a hard decision to make, but we left that little blue-eyed girl for them to raise. It seemed like the right thing to do at the time, and we hope we made the right decision. The trail was a poor place to haul an infant around, and we worried that we might not find milk along the way. The couple we left her with had cows and a nice little farm."

"You did the right thing," Matilda said softly. "Poor dear might have died on the trip, and then you'd have had that on your conscience. You gave her a fighting chance by letting that loving couple have her."

"Thank you," Fairlee said softly.

Isaac could hear tears in Fairlee's voice, so he took up the tale. "We saved another little girl too. She wasn't a baby, though. She was a tiny spitfire."

"Go on," Matilda said.

Isaac looked at Fairlee and saw tears still threatening, so he kept talking. "We came upon an Indian village and had no choice but to ride through it. The Indians had

61

kidnapped a little white girl several months before and were raising her as one of their own. She had blond hair and blue eyes, and the chief's son thought that was a good-luck talisman. They wanted to buy Delia to be the child's mother and for the son to take as a wife, but the three sisters stood up to those Indians like true troopers. Before the dust had settled, they'd traded our pack mule, complete with their supplies and nuns' habits, for the little girl, and then, lo and behold, if we didn't find her parents in the next town where we stopped."

Matilda was tickled at that and laughed so hard that she complained that her stays hurt her ribs. "I'd liked to have been a fly on the wall when the Indians found the habits. What do you reckon they did with them?"

"We kind of hoped they thought they were good-luck charms and wore them on their next raid." Fairlee giggled and discreetly swiped a hand across her eyes.

The laughter was so infectious that they were all four howling when the stage stopped and Cap opened the door. "Don't know what's so funny in here, but we'll be taking a fifteen-minute break. You ladies can head that way toward that copse of trees, and us gentlemen will go the opposite way over toward them bushes. Then we'll have

62

us some lunch. It's cold out, but it'll beat eating while we ride. Kind of hard to hit the mouth when the wheels hit ruts and shake up the whole contraption," he said.

The trip to the trees reminded Fairlee of all the times she and her sisters had raced off to the privacy of underbrush during their adventure. As she'd said, she'd thought that escapade would be her last one — had prayed that it would be — but here she was, smack-dab in the middle of another one. She hoped this one wouldn't involve Indians, orphaned babies, kidnapped children, or mantraps dug into the earth. She was glad that at least each time she took a step, her foot hit solid ground.

CHAPTER THREE

Matilda and Polly nodded off to sleep after they'd eaten their noon meal of bread and cheese. They dozed with their chins tucked down to their bosoms and their heads bobbing every time Cap hit a rut in the road. Matilda snored loudly enough to rattle the leather curtains, but Polly slept right through it. Fairlee bet they could both sleep through a tornado on a rocking boat. Possibly even with a snoring man sitting in a corner.

Fairlee drew her legs up onto the bench and wrapped her fur-lined cape tightly around them. When she leaned her head into the corner of the coach, she eyed Matilda's valise. It would make a fine pillow, but getting it out from between the two women might involve a tug-of-war. She wasn't sleepy, but it felt good to shift from a sitting position to a leaning one. Her mind grew clearer with each passing hour. That morning at breakfast she'd still been slightly dizzy, and when they'd stopped, she didn't feel quite right. But now in the mid-afternoon all the cobwebs were gone, and she could remember almost everything that had happened. At least while she was awake. That twenty-four-hour stretch that she'd slept would be gone forever.

Where was Matthew today? Was he angry? Had he rode off in a rage, searching for her to bring her home and make her honor her word that she would marry him? Or had Isaac been right, and Matthew didn't even care enough to get angry but went on to the next woman with means? She'd had a few doubts that he really, really loved her but had convinced herself that it wasn't anything but bride's jitters. After all, he was so hand-some and dashing in his fancy coats. Not at all like Isaac in his rough clothes, worn boots, and sweat-stained hat.

The sun peeked through the heavy clouds, sending slivers through the cracks of the leather curtains. Fairlee pulled back the edge of a curtain enough to see the country-side going past at a steady clip, but the bright sun didn't erase the doubts that Isaac had caused with his smart remarks.

Blast his sorry old hide to Hades forever for making her think that way. She'd get even with him if it was the last thing she ever did. He'd better watch his back once they were in Mississippi, because he had a reckoning on the way.

Walkin' on clouds, indeed! A Lavalle woman always keeps both feet on the ground and her wits about her, she thought.

You didn't for a while there. You left good sense behind and let Matthew lead you right down the daisy path, didn't you? that little voice that sounded so much like her mother's argued. *I raised you to think for yourself. When you had the first doubt about him, why didn't you simply break the engagement?*

I wanted to be married. I wanted a home and children. I didn't see a rush of men beating a path to Oak View to ask for my hand, she continued to counter.

Patience, my child. You can have it all in due time and with a man who will make you happy, not miserable, the voice in her head said and then disappeared.

Cap picked up speed, and the coach rocked back and forth as much as forward. It was worse than the ship by far. All it needed was mice and mildew, and she'd feel the same as she did when she awoke in the captain's cabin.

Captain's cabin, my hind end. I bet that was a storage room. No self-respecting captain would spend even one night in a place like that.

The next rut sent her against Isaac's side. He mumbled something in his sleep. She quickly righted herself and went back to her half of the bench. Matilda's chins bobbled, but she continued to sleep. Polly said, "Oh, Bennie, darlin'," in her sleep, and Fairlee cocked her head to one side to hear more.

"Who?" she asked softly.

"Bennie, my sweetheart. We're going to get married next week. Shh, don't tell anyone," Polly said, then opened her eyes wide and clamped a hand over her mouth.

"You talk in your sleep," Fairlee said.

"I know, and I've been so afraid that Grandmother would hear me, I've been afraid to go to sleep very soundly." Polly blushed.

"Congratulations," Fairlee said.

"Thank you. Bennie and I are going to elope before I have to go back with Grandmother. My little sister can take my place," she whispered.

"I won't say a word. Go on back to sleep. If she wakes up first, I'll kick your foot and wake you up," Fairlee whispered back.

Polly shut her eyes. "You are a good person."

She mumbled several times, and Fairlee

tried to make out the words but couldn't. Isaac added his snores to Matilda's, and Fairlee cut her eyes to her left. Like Matilda, his chin rested on his chest. Dark lashes fanned out on his high cheekbones, and his dark hair needed combing. His long legs stretched across the distance between the two benches, almost touching Polly's toes. Arms were crossed across his chest and his body drawn in as much as possible to fend off the cold drafts seeping in between the curtains.

Fairlee had no doubts about Isaac Burnet. If he said he was taking her to Delia's, then that's what would happen. If he told a woman he loved her, she could rest assured that he did and would until eternity dawned, and he'd never ask a woman to marry him to get at her money either. Fairlee didn't like the thoughts, but they were pure, unadulterated truth, and she couldn't stop them.

She snuggled deeper into her fur-lined cape, thankful to be warm. She'd traveled with Isaac for weeks back in the spring. They'd crossed horns more than once during that time, and she remembered their bickering with a smile on her face. She wondered what had happened in his world during the past several months. She'd been courted very properly by Matthew and planned a quiet wedding. After all, it wouldn't have been right to throw a lavish affair when her father hadn't been dead a year.

During all those weeks and months, what had Isaac been doing? Had he been planning a wedding back in Mississippi? If so, what was his lady friend going to think of his dashing off to Louisiana to help kidnap Delia's sister?

Suddenly the green face of jealousy reared its ugly head. She didn't want Isaac to be engaged and was angry at herself for caring. She'd only been away from Matthew for a day, and those thoughts weren't right. She shouldn't care if Isaac Burnet was engaged, married, or even courting a woman that he might possibly fall in love with in the future. It was none of her business. And yet, there was that flash of envy to prove that she did care. She was so confused that she couldn't think her way out of the maze, and that upset her even more than the jealous streak.

Isaac slowly lowered his hand to his belt, where he kept a knife in a sheath. Instinct told him danger was near. Were Indians chasing him, or was he only dreaming? Wary, he opened his eyes barely a slit and realized that he was in the stagecoach, and just like that the nightmares were gone. Matilda Greenly and Polly were still asleep. He turned his head toward Fairlee to find her snuggled down in her cape with her eyes shut. Thick, dark lashes fanned out across her flawless cheeks. No wonder Matthew Cheval wanted her. The money would keep him for a while until he went through every dime with his gambling and womanizing habits, but Fairlee would look really good on his arm when he needed a wife at his side.

Fairlee had been staring at Isaac and barely had time to snap her eyelids shut when he glanced her way. Pretending to be asleep was difficult. She'd never been good at it. Her nose itched. Her foot went to sleep. Her toes twitched. Isaac had no business waking up at the very moment she was studying his face to see if she could determine whether or not he had a fiancée or even the prospects of one. Leave it to a man to wake up at precisely the wrong moment.

She slowly counted to sixty and then fluttered her eyes open. "When did you awaken?" she whispered.

His gaze quickly shifted around the dark interior of the stage. "A couple of minutes ago. We should be there soon. The sun is

70

starting to set, and we've made good time. We'll enjoy sleeping in inns for the next few nights. After that we'll be on the road and sleeping wherever we can find a place, much like the trip from Texas to Louisiana."

"Where will I get a horse?" she asked.

"We'll buy one in Monroe, along with a pack animal to carry supplies, which we will also buy in Monroe," he answered.

"I get to choose the horse," she said.

"I thought you could ride anything that had four legs." He pointedly reminded her of a boast she'd made on their last trip together.

"You remembered — how sweet," she smarted off at him.

"Don't be sassy with me, wo— Fairlee." He corrected himself in the middle of the word. There was no need to aggravate her any further. Besides, he rather liked her smiles better than her frowns.

"We'll get you a horse, and I have no doubt you'll keep up quite well. Promise me right now that you won't turn around and run back to Cheval once you have a chance to ride," he whispered.

She sighed and nodded. "I have decided that going to Delia's is in my best interest. If you drop dead on the road, I'll still go to Delia's. Matthew deserves more than a tainted woman. You've ruined my life, and I can't help that, Isaac. But Delia had a big hand in it, and she's going to hear what I've got to say. I'd ride through Indians and the blazes of hell to tell her what I think of her stunt."

Polly sat up with a start and rubbed her eyes. "Who's Delia? And did you just say a bad word?"

"I did, and I'd say it again. Delia is my older sister. She married Isaac's cousin, and we're going to see her," Fairlee said quickly.

Polly rolled her neck to get the kinks out. "That will be nice."

Fairlee nodded. "It might be, after the fight."

"I'm so excited that I get to see my sister, I sure wouldn't fight with her," Polly said.

"She didn't ruin your life, did she?" Fairlee asked.

Polly settled in and got ready for another story. "Oh, no. Tell me more."

Fairlee looked out the window. "Not about this. I'm not sure I could put into words just how angry I am at both of my sisters."

Delia would think that the devil's daughter had come through hell's blazes when Fairlee got finished with her, and that was giving her sister the short end of the deal to boot, because Fairlee intended to live with her forever. She had made up her mind in the last twenty-four hours that she was never traveling again. Delia could just deal with that, and if she didn't like it, Fairlee would be glad to remind her that she was the cause of her not being married and living in Louisiana. At least no one would know her in Mississippi to whisper about her behind their hands.

There's Delia Fannin's sister. I heard she's a wanton wench. Traveled across country with men she didn't even know once, and then went on another trip with a man without a proper chaperone. I sure wouldn't want my brother — or *son* or *nephew* or *uncle,* whichever fit the case — *married to her.*

"They can go kiss Lucifer right smack on his forked little tail," she mumbled.

"What about a tail?" Polly asked.

Fairlee blushed. She'd forgotten about the other three people in the stage.

Before she could answer, the stagecoach came to an abrupt halt. Polly had to grab the side of the bench to keep from tumbling over into Isaac's lap. Matilda shook her head and looked around. "What are we stopping for? Indians? Did we get stuck?"

Polly was so excited, she slung open the stage door before Cap could dismount from

the top of the coach. "We're here, Grandmother!"

"Well, that's wonderful, even though I will
miss the stories you young folks entertained
us with. I would have liked to hear more,
but I'm glad we have arrived. I don't like
this fast means of travel. I don't like travel
at all, but to go to sleep in my bed one night
and sleep in a different one twenty miles
away the next night isn't natural."

Cap set the steps beside the door and held
out his hand for Polly. Seeing her smooth
young fingers in his ropey old ones was like
looking at the past and future entangled
together, Fairlee reflected. Fairlee had a
past, but she wondered about her future.
Polly had both all tied up with a red ribbon.
For a moment she envied the girl her
Bennie and the excitement of eloping, then
beginning a new life with the man she loved.

"Had a good trip, didn't we?" Cap re-
marked. "I was afraid it was going to rain
and get all muddy, and we'd get stuck a few
times, but we made the best time me and
old Shooter have done in many a moon.
This stage will be going on to the next stop
as soon as we change horses and get something to eat. You two coming with us?" Cap
looked at Isaac.

"I expect we'll stay on here until tomorrow. What time does the next stage come through in the morning?"

"Have to ask the station manager. I'm not sure about the schedule tomorrow. We'll be pulling out in an hour if you change your mind," Cap said. "I'll wait 'til the last minute to tell Shooter to unload your trunk."

"Thank you," Isaac said.

A bitter north wind pushed him and Fairlee across the yard to the porch of a local inn and flipped her cape around her ankles, almost tripping her in the rush. Warmth and the smell of fresh-baked bread poured out when he opened the door. The place was filled with the noise of several conversations, and Fairlee sighed. The tables could accommodate barely a dozen people, and there were already nine there before Matilda and Polly joined the crowd, leaving Isaac and Fairlee to sit at the last available table.

Two families occupied nearby tables, one with two small children, the other with five youngsters ranging in age from about five to twelve or thirteen. Fairlee wondered if they were traveling by coach or if they'd just stopped on their journey, perhaps by wagon train, for a hot meal. The children all looked clean, and their shoes were polished, which made her think they were stagecoach riders and not wagon train folks. The latter would have dust on them everywhere from walking beside the wagons, and even at this time of year not all the children would likely have shoes.

"Oh, no!" Fairlee muttered.

Isaac scanned the room for everything from a rat to Matthew Cheval. "What?"

"Remember what that innkeeper said? This place has only two rooms to let. Two families are already here, and no more coaches except the one we were on will be leaving tonight. These families don't look the type to travel half the night with small children in tow, do they?" she said.

Isaac groaned. "Guess we'll be sleeping in chairs again tonight."

"Not me. If I can't have a bed, I'd just as soon be traveling," she said.

Isaac's face registered disappointment. "I'd looked forward to a night in a bed with a real pillow under my head."

She smiled. "Doing without is your punishment for ruining my life."

He sat back so fast that his chair rocked. "You are downright mean, Fairlee Lavalle."

She eased back in her chair and shook the cape from her shoulders. "What I am is hungry."

A woman with a strong resemblance to both Matilda Greenly and her granddaughter hustled from the kitchen to their table. "Excuse me for being so slow, but I had to greet my daughter, Polly, and my mother. They tried to tell me your story, but it'll have to wait. I've got hot beef soup and fresh bread, some cheese, and a peach cobbler for dessert. That all right?"

"What about rooms for the night?" Fairlee asked.

She shook her head. "Too late. Those two families have already taken the rooms. They'll be wall-to-wall with young'uns on pallets. One family is going south on the eight o'clock in the morning. The other one is going east on the nine o'clock. Want to sleep in the dining room beside the fire tonight and rent a room as soon as they're out?"

Fairlee shook her head. "No, we'll just have a good hot meal and go on to the next stop with the stage that we came in on. How long will that take us, do you think?"

"If you make good time and encounter no bad weather, you might make it by daybreak. Want me to fix you up a little snack in case you get hungry or don't make it by breakfast time?" she asked.

"That would be very nice," Fairlee said.

Cap and Shooter came in from outside and looked around. The couple with the two small children had just started up the stairs. Cap motioned toward the table, and Shooter followed him. Half a loaf of bread had been left behind with the dirty dishes. Cap picked it up and pulled it into two pieces with his hands. He gave half to Shooter and poured honey from a quart jar onto his piece. He stacked up the used dishes as he ate, pushing them to one side.

A young woman brought two big bowls of soup and set them before Fairlee and Isaac. She hurried back to the kitchen and brought out a loaf of bread, a plate of sliced cheese, and two bowls of cobbler on a tray.

"We'll have whatever you're givin' them folks." Cap raised his voice above the din of the other table.

"Yes, you will, because that's all we got tonight," the young woman said with a laugh.

"Then it's a dang good thing we like soup and cheese," Shooter flirted.

"Ah, Shooter, you'd eat shoe leather with gravy on top of it and say it was good. You need to find a wife," she teased.

"Not this old cowboy. A wife would only slow me down. Besides, I done asked you to marry me a dozen times, and you always say no. Your husband's been dead now a year, so it wouldn't be improper," he said.

She turned at the kitchen door. "I'll marry you tomorrow if you quit that stage business."

"See there? Always got to try to change a man. Women don't realize that men is men, and whatever they is ain't goin' to be changed." Shooter poured honey onto the final bite of his bread and popped it into his mouth.

"Amen," Isaac said.

Fairlee cut her eyes at him. "Don't you even start."

"I didn't say it. Shooter did. I just agreed. You got a bone to pick, do it with him. I'm too tired to listen to you nag," he said.

"Don't you be giving me the name if you don't want the game. I'll show you what nagging is if you say that again," Fairlee said.

He held up his palms. "Don't shoot me just because I agreed with the fellow. You want a hot meal, you'd best get at it. I don't think they'll hold the stage if you aren't finished."

She shot him a look meant to drop him into nothing more than a greasy spot on the floor, and set about eating the best soup she'd had in weeks. He smiled at her, which raised her ire even higher and made her eat faster. Anything to get away from the table with him, when everyone thought they were married. She wouldn't be married to Isaac Burnet for all the money in the world or all the dirt in Texas. She wouldn't vow to love him until death parted them if someone offered her . . . she couldn't think of a single thing big enough or important enough to coerce her into being his real wife.

Not even if he told you he loved you? that irritating voice inside her head asked.

That would be mixing hot bacon grease and water. Nothing but a burning explosion, she argued.

Fairlee hung on to the edge of the bench with one hand, but it was a futile attempt to keep from tumbling onto the floor. If she was going to get a wink of sleep, she might as well give up and curl up on the coach floor. The trouble was that Isaac had forsaken the bench for the floor within the first ten minutes of their leaving, and she could not make herself sleep that close to him.

She sat up, trying to get comfortable by shoving herself into a corner and leaning her head back. Shooter wasn't as good at missing ruts and potholes as Cap had been. Maybe it was because it was dark, with the moon and stars obliterated by clouds, or maybe it was simply because he didn't drive as much as Cap. The next rough spot he hit sent her into a bounce that bumped her head on the top of the stage and set her back down with such force that she'd probably have a bruise on her backside the next morning.

Isaac groaned and rolled over with his back to her. She coveted his spot on the floor and wished she'd thought of it before he did. Then he'd be sitting up wide awake, so sleepy he couldn't hold his eyes open with sewing needles. He'd traveled at night before, and he knew, the rogue, to forsake the benches and curl up on the floor. He stopped snoring and wedged himself under her bench.

She set her mouth in a firm line and looked at the remaining floor space. No one would ever know that she'd slept with a man that close. Besides, everyone thought they were married, so if Cap or Shooter saw them together, it would be perfectly fine. She eased off the bench, stepping over Isaac, and stretched out on the floor.

"Ah," she sighed. She turned her back to him, wrapped up in her cape like a butterfly in a cocoon, and promptly fell asleep, the stage rocking her the way her mother had when she was small.

The abrupt stillness awoke her. She sat up to find Isaac already on a bench, staring right at her. It took but a few seconds for her to claim the other bench and push errant strands of hair out of her face. If they didn't find a place to stop and freshen up soon, every bit of her bun was going to sneak out from the pins that held it in a chignon at the nape of her neck.

"Bad news!" Cap yelled before he opened the door.

"What now?" Fairlee moaned.

He threw open the door, and she didn't need an explanation. The stage station they had just reached was in smoldering ruins, with not a thing left but the fireplace. "Happened yesterday. Horses are fine — fire didn't get the barn. Station owner is sleeping out there in the tack room. We can change them out, but there won't be any breakfast other than whatever you got with you. We'll go on to the next stop soon as the horses are changed. Guess y'all will be traveling with us again?"

"What choice do we have?" Fairlee asked.

Cap spat a stream of tobacco juice onto the ground. "Not much."

"How much farther to the next station?" Isaac asked.

"Only half as far as these last two. They

got a pretty nice inn up there. Got several rooms upstairs to let out and good food. We ought to be there by noon," he said.

"You and Shooter got any food? We can share what we have left," Fairlee offered.

"Naw, thanks. We had Rosy make us up a poke of leftovers at the last stop. I got some good sleep up against your big old trunk on top while Shooter drove, so now he can sleep to the next stop. We get all the way to Monroe, we have a layover for a night, and we can get some real rest. But I'm much obliged at the offer. Ain't everyone who'd worry about us old men." He grinned.

"You are very welcome," she said.

"Mr. Burnet, you be good to that woman. She's a keeper," Cap said. "Y'all want to stretch them legs out? We'll be here about fifteen minutes."

"I would like that," Fairlee said. If she didn't find some privacy soon, she was going to be in big trouble. As soon as Cap set the steps up beside the stage, she headed toward the outhouse at a steady clip. She didn't care if it was improper for her to be racing. It was that or dragging that trunk down for a fresh pair of pantaloons.

Isaac fed and watered his horse during the stop. Poor thing hadn't had much rest since

Isaac had mounted up and left Greenville almost three weeks before. Isaac whispered into the horse's ear, "When we get to Monroe, I promise you a whole day of rest before we take off again. And this is the last time you'll have to keep going night and day. That's not fair, and I'm sorry."

"Sorry about what?" Fairlee asked.

Her voice startled him, and he jumped. "That my poor old horse has had to keep going night and day without proper rest."

"You apologize to a horse? *I've* kept going without proper rest, and I was kidnapped, and I'm doing it against my will, so why don't you apologize to me?" she snapped.

"Because I'm doing you a favor. You're just too dang stubborn to admit it." He walked off in the direction of the outhouse.

The innkeeper brought the fresh horses around and helped harness them up. "I'm very sorry about this, ma'am. I understand you and your husband rode all night with hopes of staying in my inn. It was a nice place, and I'll rebuild, but it'll take a while. Maybe if you come back through here next year, we'll be ready for guests. Until then I'll make do in the barn loft, and it'll just be a stop instead of a layover."

"Isn't your fault, sir. And I'm sorry for your misfortune." She climbed back into the stage and settled into her corner. The wooden seat felt ten times more uncomfortable than it had earlier, the leather curtains a hundred times uglier, and the dismay in her heart a thousand times greater.

Isaac and the men talked when he returned. She caught snatches of their conversation — something about the horse being a good one to hold up to that kind of traveling and about Isaac's having a right nice little wife. They could talk about boiling potatoes or picking chicken feathers for all she cared. She just wanted a bath, a hairbrush, and a nice soft bed.

Isaac finally took his place across from her. "Are you pouting?"

Just as he spoke, the stage gave a lurch, and they were off again, bouncing up and down with every rut and hole in their path. Fairlee suddenly looked forward to riding a horse all day and sleeping wherever they could find shelter. Anything beat hard wooden seats and being cooped up with Isaac.

"I am not pouting." She pulled back the curtain enough to see outside. A soft mist fell, creating a depressing gray tint only slightly less dense than heavy fog. Every now and then she caught sight of an illusive tree, and once she saw a deer running away from the noisy coach.

She was doing the right thing, going to Delia's place, but it sure grated on her nerves to think about the rest of the trip ahead. She liked a house, a soft mattress, digging in the flower beds, and even doing laundry. She wasn't the Lavalle sister who craved adventure, even though it kept landing right smack-dab in her lap.

Isaac dug around in the poke Rosy had made for them and brought out bread and cheese. He broke off a hunk of bread and used his knife to cut a wedge of cheese from the small round. "Want something?"

She nodded and held out her hand. He handed her the poke. "Help yourself."

"Knife?"

He raised an eyebrow. "You don't carry your own?"

"Usually I keep one on my belt, but if you'll remember, I was about to go to bed when you kidnapped me. My knife is probably still lying on the vanity in my room," she reminded him.

He handed her his knife. "Promise you'll use it for cheese only and won't slit my throat with it?"

"What a pleasant idea."

"Ah, come on, Fairlee. You've had plenty of time to get over the fact that you aren't going to be a bride. From what I hear, the Cheval place is falling down around Matthew's ears. Your dowry wouldn't have begun to make it whole again, and he probably wouldn't even use the money to make it livable anyway — he'd have gambled it away."

She stared at him. "You don't know that. You're just guessing."

He looked at her but made no reply. Finally he said softly, "Don't stay mad the whole trip. It's long enough without us being hateful to each other."

She cut a wedge from the cheese and handed it back to him. Their hands brushed in the transfer, and his touch made tingles race up and down her arms. Fairlee rolled her eyes. She refused to let Isaac affect her that way. She'd given her heart to Matthew Cheval, and she hadn't had time to get over him. There was no way she would ever admit that she was even faintly attracted to a man of Isaac's caliber. He was an outlaw and a kidnapper, for God's sake.

Don't you be taking the Lord's name in vain, Fairlee, or I'll wash your mouth out with soap. Her mother's voice was as clear in her ears as if she'd been sitting beside her on the bench.

She tilted her chin up in defiance. She'd

earned the right to take anyone's name in vain the past few days.

"What are you thinking about?" Isaac asked.

"Why?"

"You looked as if you were arguing with someone."

"If I look outside, I'm pouting. If I look up at the ceiling, I'm arguing. This is going to be one long blasted trip," she said.

"Hey, don't get all prickly with me. I've already been on the road almost three weeks. You haven't even had a whole week yet. Besides, you were the one who said you could outride and outshoot me," he said.

No other man in her circle of friends had ever talked to her the way Isaac Burnet did. The others were sweet and kind and mannerly. Even if they wouldn't want her as a wife, at parties they would ask her to dance or go fetch punch or tea for her. She almost snorted at the idea of Isaac behaving nicely at a party.

Stop being so snide. He behaved quite nicely at that dinner party last spring when the three of them got you home safely. Her mother's whisper in her ear sounded so clear that Fairlee wondered where it had come from.

She didn't look up or around. A book

could be compiled with the sayings and teachings Rosetta Lavalle had left behind when she passed on. Just as a separate one could be written about the things Captain Robert Lavalle had taught his daughters. Between the two parents, the girls weren't lacking in social graces or survival skills.

"You got that look again," Isaac said.

"It's dark in here. How can you tell how I'm looking?"

"It's the attitude. The way you go all stiff and proper-like."

"I could've sworn I heard my mother arguing with me, and that's not possible. She passed a year ago," Fairlee said honestly.

"I do the same thing. My dad argues with me all the time, especially when I'm about to mess up," he said.

"When was the last time?" she asked.

Isaac chuckled. "When I told Delia to send Micah instead of me to get you. Dad really had something to say about that. He said I was about to make a mistake. I told him that I'd had all the running across the country I wanted, but he wouldn't give me a minute's peace until I went back and told Delia I'd go. He said Delia was a good woman, and if she wanted you to come to Mississippi, I was going after you," Isaac said.

"Wonder why?" Fairlee murmured.

Her face was beautiful when she pondered a question like that. Isaac wished she would always look so sweet.

Isaac chuckled again. "He had a strange sense of humor. If he was alive, he'd be laughing his fool head off right about now."

"So would my mother."

They hit a rut that sent her sliding across the bench and straight into Isaac's lap. The force knocked him backward, and his rear end slid out of the seat. They both landed on the floor of the stage in a tangle of arms, legs, knees, and elbows.

The shock of his hand touching her fingertips as he tried to put them both to rights made her angrier than the fall. Life had been good to her sister Delia. Why did it have to be so rotten to her?

"Y'all all right back there?" Cap yelled.

"Fine!" Isaac hollered back, as he righted himself and helped Fairlee up to the bench.

"Good. Thought I heard you both rollin' around like stones in a glass jar!" he shouted. "Road is getting slick. We might be an hour longer."

Fairlee wanted to cry, but even if it meant going before a firing squad in her under-clothing, she wouldn't let Isaac see a single tear trail down her cheek. She was a Lavalle woman, and they were as tough as buffalo hide. She set her jaw to keep her chin from quivering.

Isaac was no stranger to battling an attraction to Fairlee Lavalle. He'd felt it all the way back when he'd thought she was a nun and had to really talk to himself about such a horrible thing. Then when she wasn't a nun anymore, he'd felt his heart stirring toward her. But they'd parted ways after Bennet's Bluff, and he'd thought time and space would help him overcome the crazy feeling. He refused to act on the itchy sensation down deep in his heart and soul. Fairlee Lavalle was entirely too sharp-tongued for him. He wanted a nice, sweet wife who didn't argue with him at every tick of the clock.

And you'll be bored to death before a year is out with a woman like that, son, his father's voice said, so close to his ear that he whipped his head around to make sure the old fellow wasn't sitting beside him. *Like Delia, Fairlee'd keep you on your toes, and you'd never be bored. She reminds me of your mother.*

"We should be able to get rooms at the next stop," he said aloud to Fairlee, "since we'll be arriving there so early. You can sleep all day and night. We'll plan on leaving early tomorrow morning on the first stage going east," he added. But he knew he was talking to himself as much as or more than to Fairlee. A day and a half away from keeping such close company with her would help him get his priorities back into order and his perspective in line again. And, with luck, his father's voice wouldn't torment him anymore. He was tired, hungry, and aching for a bed. When he was rested, fed, and feeling human again, surely Fairlee wouldn't be nearly the temptation that she was right then.

"If *that* place is burned to the ground, I'm sleeping in the barn with the animals," she declared.

"And if the barn is burned too?" he asked.

"Then I'll find a cedar tree and sleep under it. I'm so tired of movement I could . . ." She paused.

"What? You could what?"

"I could take that knife and whittle this contraption into kindling for a campfire."

"Then I guess we'd best hope the next station is standing and has a couple of rooms." He chuckled.

"Don't laugh at me. All I wanted was to stay at home and never leave again."

"That's all I wanted too. Guess neither of us got our wish."

CHAPTER FOUR

Dark clouds still blocked out any sunlight when Cap brought the stage to a halt in front of a small station not much bigger than the San Antonio jail where Isaac had felt so cooped up. He dreaded going inside. There was no way that tiny building had rooms to let, and Fairlee was going to throw a pure old hissy fit. And if by some chance the inn did have rooms, they would be so small, it would be like sleeping in a pantry.

Fairlee knew that her face must be the picture of pure bewilderment as she looked at the rough-hewn log building before them. If only she had her own horse, she'd stop riding the stage right then and light out on her own. Sleeping on a bed of leaves or even on the dirt with the moon and stars above wouldn't be as bad as trying to rest in a bouncing coach, and she couldn't imagine the little building in front of her having anything more than a dining room and kitchen.

Give me a horse, and I'll point my internal compass toward the north. If Isaac doesn't like it, he can keep riding the stage and have the whole danged floor to himself.

If ifs *and* buts *were candy and nuts . . .* She heard her mother's old adage.

"We'd all be smiling," Fairlee finished for her mother.

"What did you say?" Isaac asked.

"I hope they've got something hot cooked up," she answered. She wasn't getting into a long-winded explanation of why she'd made that statement. Mercy, she hadn't even realized she was talking aloud until she heard her own voice.

A tall, lanky man about Cap's size opened the front door of the station and hurried to the stage. "I heard that the station up the way burned to the ground. Reckon y'all are tired travelers. Catherina has beans and ham ready. Head on in, and she'll serve you right up. I'll get the horses changed out for you, Cap."

"Good to see you, Etienne. Got Isaac and Fairlee Burnet here. They've had bad luck with inns," Cap agreed.

"You got rooms?" Isaac asked.

"Got one. It's empty. Talk to Catherina." Etienne started taking care of the horses.

"It's mine," Fairlee whispered.

Isaac ignored her and looked at the station man. "I'll pay extra for you to feed, water, and put my horse in a stall until tomorrow."

"Need your saddlebags brought inside?"

"That would be good," Isaac said.

"It's a fine animal. Interested in selling him?"

"No, sir, I'm not. He's been good to me, and he belonged to my father. I couldn't sell him."

Etienne nodded seriously. "I understand. Take your pretty young bride into the house and feed her before she faints plumb away. You look weary and hungry," he said to her.

"I am," Fairlee admitted.

Catherina met them in the middle of the dining room floor. She was as tall and slender as her husband, had dark brown hair, going to gray, pulled back into a tight knot at the nape of her neck, and wrinkles deep enough to hide small children in. But when she smiled, the whole room lit up in spite of the dreary weather.

"Come in. Come in. So glad to see you, Cap. I made your favorite today. Big old smoked ham, beans, fried sweet potatoes, and even a thick apple pie. Who'd you bring with you?" Catherina asked.

"Young married couple we picked up in St. Charles. They were going to stay over at the first stop, but the rooms were all full. Then when we stopped yesterday, the station had caught fire and burned down. I think they're tired to the bone of the stagecoach. You got anyone in that room you let out?"

Catherina patted Fairlee on the back the whole way to the table. "Not a soul. Bless your hearts. Come on and sit, sweet. We'll have you fed in no time. Want me to put on a kettle of water so you can have a bath? I'll put the tub in your room if you'd like. Mercy, but I bet your poor little bones are weary."

Fairlee untied her cape and draped it over the back of her chair. "Thank you. I'd love a bath, and then I'm going to sleep until tomorrow morning. What time does the stage going east leave?"

"Late this evening we get one, then midmorning tomorrow," Catherina answered.

Isaac removed his coat and hung it over the back of his chair. "We'll take the one tomorrow morning and keep the room until then."

Cap and Shooter went to the kitchen and served up their own plates. They carried them to a table on the other side of the room and tucked into the hot meal with gusto.

"Good ham," Cap told Catherina.

"Etienne makes wine in the summertime, and I use a little when I bake the ham," she said. "It makes it tender. I'll go and get your dinner," she told Fairlee and Isaac.

"They're French," Fairlee said.

"Does that make a difference?"

"I'm just making a statement. And I'm not sleeping in that room with you, and you are not staying in there while I take my bath."

"We *are* married," he reminded her.

"No, we are not."

At the sharpness of their voices, Cap and Shooter stopped talking and stared. Blessedly, they hadn't heard her actual words.

"Shine already worn off the honeymoon?" Cap asked.

"It's getting pretty dull," Fairlee said.

"Get some rest. That'll make it all bright again," Shooter said.

Catherina returned with two plates, forks, knives, and spoons and set them on the table. "You fix those, and I'll bring food."

Fairlee set the table, and Catherina made three trips. First with a platter of ham and a bowl of beans, next with a bowl of sweet potatoes and a plate of biscuits, and the third with two cups of steaming hot coffee.

"You take cream or sugar?"

Fairlee and Isaac both shook their heads.

"I agree. That ruins good coffee. When you finish your meal, your bath will be ready. Maybe your good-looking husband will want one when you finish. He's a big, strong man — he can pull the tub out into the hall when he is finished, and Etienne will take care of it. Then you can rest in a feather bed as long as you want. Too much riding in one of those contraptions makes for raw nerves. Eat, *chéris*. Don't be shy."

Catherina hurried back to the kitchen to slice pie for Cap and Shooter.

" 'Shy,' my hind end." Isaac forked a large piece of ham onto his plate.

"You are so rude," Fairlee said.

"Maybe so, but I'm honest. There's not a shy bone in a Lavalle. And I'm having a bath when you get done. We might not get another chance for days," he said.

"I can't imagine being really married to an outlaw like you."

"I'm not an outlaw, and, sweetheart, you've got nothing to worry about. I wouldn't marry a Lavalle if God promised me a front seat in heaven for the deed."

"You were in jail, and you kidnapped me. That makes you an outlaw. And don't use

98

endearments when you talk to me. I'm not your 'sweetheart.' "

"Did wearing a habit make you a nun?" he asked.

"Of course not!" She raised her voice from a whisper to a near shout. Both Cap and Shooter looked their way again with grins on their faces.

"I rest my case."

"You are . . ." She realized they had an audience. ". . . not a lawyer. You can't 'rest your case.' I'm tired of fighting with you."

He stared at her as if she had two heads and eighteen eyeballs.

She whispered so low that only his ears caught it. "And if you believe that, you are stupid as well as an outlaw."

"Ready for pie?" Catherina called from the kitchen door.

"Can you fix one up for me and Cap to take along for later?" Shooter asked through the mouthful of apples he was already chewing.

Fairlee shook her head. "May I please have mine to take to the room for later?"

Catherina's brown eyes sparkled. "Of course."

"I'll take one piece now and one for later," Isaac said.

Catherina carried a whole pie, sliced into

six sections and loosely wrapped, to Shooter and Cap, and a separate piece on a plate to Isaac. When she passed Fairlee's chair, she leaned down and whispered, "I'll put two pieces in your room. Goodlookin' as your husband is, you might work up an appetite, *ma petite.*"

A blush stung Fairlee's cheeks so fiercely, they felt as if the embers from the fireplace had scorched them.

Isaac dug into his huge piece of pie. "What did she say?"

"None of your business, and nothing that's bound to happen," Fairlee said.

He shoved a forkful of warm apple pie toward her so fast that she opened her mouth without thinking. "Have a bite? Good, ain't it?" he said.

She nodded. "Almost as good as Fanny's."

Cap and Shooter finished their dessert moments before Etienne stomped across the porch, wiped his feet, and hurried in out of the dreary cold. "You are all ready to go. Horses are changed out. The tired ones are fed and watered as well as your horse, Mr. Burnet. Want I should put your saddlebags in your room?"

"I'd be obliged," Isaac said.

Etienne carried them through a door beside the fireplace that Fairlee hadn't even noticed. He left the door open, and she could see two beds, a rocking chair between them, room for her trunk at the end of one, and space enough for a bathing tub at the end of the other. In the far left corner was a washstand with bath sheets and washcloths folded on top of it.

"My trunk?" she asked.

"Shooter will put it into the room for you," Cap said. "Maybe we'll see you again. Been a pleasure driving you. Most women whine a lot more than you did."

"Thank you!" Fairlee smiled.

"You are a lucky man, Mr. Burnet," Cap said.

Isaac searched his heart and soul and couldn't come up with an answer, so he just nodded and shook Cap's hand.

Shooter carried the trunk in on his shoulders and had to duck to get it through the door. He set it inside the room at the end of the bed on the left, then returned to the dining room and stopped at their table.

"Good-bye to you. Here's hoping you many happy years, lots of pretty little girls to give their daddy fits, and handsome, mischievous boys to steal their momma's heart. That's a good old Irish wedding blessing, but it seems to work here as well."

"Thank you, Shooter." Fairlee almost

choked on the words. This pretend world was a whole lot tougher to stomach than the real one. All she had to do was tell Shooter and Cap that Isaac had kidnapped her. They'd string him up and make sure she had an escort back home. But doubts about Matthew kept her mouth closed.

Etienne appeared out of the kitchen with a metal, oval-shaped tub and put it in the bedroom. He made two trips with kettles of boiling water, then several more with buckets of cold water. Catherina came out to test the water and make him bring two more of boiling water before she declared it the right temperature for Fairlee. She laid soap on the rocking chair and winked when she passed the table where they were still sitting.

"There's my special rose soap. It'll make you think of spring. If you need anything else, *ma petite,* you just ask. A woman shouldn't have to go as long as you did without the comforts of a bedroom. Mr. Burnet, don't you let her fall asleep in that water and catch pneumonia." She shook an index finger at Isaac.

"No, ma'am. I will see to it that she doesn't."

Crimson crept from Fairlee's neck to her cheeks. "Thank you for a lovely meal,

Catherina. I'm going to go right now and take advantage of that warm water and soft bed. If I sleep past supper and awake in the night, I'll have that wonderful pie for a snack."

"If you wake up hungry, you go to the kitchen, and there will be bread and cheese waiting for you," Catherina said. "I'll get that pie for you to take to your room right now."

"Thank you again." Fairlee picked up her cape and carried it to the room. She left the door ajar and opened her trunk. The night before her wedding day it had been filled with new things for the new bride in the new plantation house that was to be her home. When she opened it now, she wasn't totally surprised to find that it was stuffed with very different things. Her riding trousers and shirts. Boots. Another coat better for riding than her fancy cape. The trunk, she knew, would be traded or sold when they left behind the stage line and rode their horses. Tempie had known that when she did the repacking, and for that Fairlee was grudgingly grateful. She was a bit surprised that Tempest had left her one decent dress and the cape, but those two items didn't mean that her younger sister wasn't in more trouble than she could wiggle out of.

Catherina handed Isaac the pie. He reached for it with one hand and picked up his coat with the other. "Thank you," he said.

"Such a nice couple. A rest will do your wife much good. She will be a different woman in the morning."

"I hope so. Fairlee is very tired."

"She has a nice name. A beautiful one to go with a beautiful woman. You are blessed," Catherina told him.

Again he nodded. Being pretend married was the hardest job he'd ever had. He'd probably have to grow a new tongue when he got back to Greenville, because he'd sure bitten his off more than once already. Why hadn't he figured out another way to travel with Fairlee? It came to him as he shut the door that he could have said he was her brother the first time someone thought they were married. It would have been a heck of a lot easier than being her husband. But hindsight's perfect vision didn't do him any good right then, when she was eyeing that warm bath with those pretty blue eyes. And a brother wouldn't have been allowed to sleep in the same room with her, so a husband he was, at least until they got home. By then he might never be a husband again. A month with a Lavalle woman would be enough to keep him a bachelor for the rest of his natural-born days.

"You're a lucky woman. There are two beds," he said.

"If there hadn't been, you would have been on the floor."

Tempie had put in an old nightgown and dressing robe. Not the fancy lace-trimmed one that had been made especially for Matthew but one that she'd worn for years. She was determined that she would not blush again as she laid it out on the bed, but she couldn't bring herself to take her undergarments from the trunk and let Isaac look upon them.

"Nope," Isaac replied. "But I would have been a gentleman and put pillows between us so as not to touch you," he added.

"You wouldn't have even been in the bed if there hadn't been two. Now sit down in that rocking chair and face the window while I have my bath. I'll do the same when you take yours. You turn around for anything, and you are a dead man. And that, sir, is a promise, not an empty threat."

"What are you going to kill me with?"

"I'll drown your sorry hide in the bathwater and swear you died of natural causes," she declared.

With a deep chuckle he sat down in the

rocker and faced the window. She didn't have a thing to worry about. He didn't want to see her anyway — not in a bath, not in a stage, not on a horse. He didn't have a choice in the matter for the most part during this journey, but that afternoon he did.

She unlaced her shoes and set them to one side, peeled off her stockings and pantaloons, untied her petticoat, and draped them all over the open trunk lid. It took a while to unfasten all the buttons down the front of her dress, and she stared at the back of Isaac's head for a long time before she actually shrugged out of it.

Isaac had never given up that easily on the last trip, or on this one so far either. What did he have up his sleeve? Was he just waiting for her to get into the tub, naked as the day she was born, and then invent a reason to turn the chair around?

His head bobbled a couple of times and then dropped. In minutes his snores filled the room. She smiled. No one, not even Isaac, could pretend that well. He'd fallen asleep. That meant she could have a nice long bath without worry. She finished undressing and stepped into the warm water, sinking down until she was covered. She undid her hair and laid the pins on the floor beside the tub. She ducked under the water and picked up the cake of soap Catherina had left beside the drying sheets. It did indeed smell like roses and reminded her of springtime. She almost broke out into song as she lathered her hair and then ducked under the water to rinse it.

When she came up for air, it was all she could do to keep from giggling aloud, just thinking about Isaac Burnet having to take a bath in rose-scented water. That would be a forerunner of the punishment he could expect for destroying her life. She began to devise wicked ways to make him pay during the next few weeks. She'd promised that she wouldn't try to escape, but by the time they reached their destination, he might be wishing she had.

She took her time soaping her body and rinsing it off, then lying back in the water and letting the warmth soak into her aching bones. Every time the snoring stopped, she shot a look in that direction to make sure Isaac was still sleeping. Finally, when the water was cool, she stood up and reached for a drying sheet, wrapped it firmly around her body, and brushed out her long dark hair. When she had most of the tangles out, she carefully rubbed it dry with the edge of the sheet. Then she hurriedly dressed in undergarments and the white cotton gown and dressing robe.

She tapped Isaac on the shoulder. "Your turn."

He awoke with a jerk and grabbed for his knife. "What?"

"Stop snoring. I'll take the chair now," she said.

"I do not snore," he said stoically as he stood up and stretched.

His mouth went as dry as if he had been eating dirt when he looked at her in all that billowing white cotton. She could have been an angel with long, flowing black hair and blue eyes. But Isaac knew Fairlee Lavalle, and she did not have a halo or fluffy white wings. He could never be tricked into believing she was an angel, not even if *he* was walking on clouds and saw her coming toward him dressed like she was right then.

She sat down in the rocker and started it moving with her bare toes. "You *do* snore, but then, so does Tempie, so it doesn't bother me. You really are lucky, because if it did keep me awake, you'd be sleeping on one of those tables out there in the dining room. Water is getting cold. If you are truly wanting a bath, you'd best get with it. If not, then I'm going to crawl in under that quilt and go to sleep. Your choice."

"I'm having a bath, and you'd better be as

accommodating as I was," he said.

"That's not a problem. I don't care to see you in the bathtub. I'd just as soon never have had to look at you again after last spring. So take your bath so I can go to bed."

It was awkward to strip down to bare skin with Fairlee only a few feet away. Even if she was turned away from him, he felt exposed and embarrassed. He quickly got into the water and gasped.

"You used up every drop of warmth. You are evil," he said.

"Matter of opinion, sir."

"Gospel truth, ma'am."

She yawned. "Shouldn't take you too long, then. I'm eager to go to bed, so hurry."

Isaac vowed that he'd stay in the water as long as he could stand the chill, just to make her wait. "I've taken cold baths before. It's no big thing. Just surprised me. Good God, what is this smell?"

Fairlee smiled brightly. "Roses. Isn't it wonderful? How could Catherina have known that I love the smell of roses in the springtime?"

"It's the middle of winter. Didn't she bring any plain old soap?"

"No, only rose-scented. You'll smell like a dandy for the next couple of days."

Isaac grinned. Two could play the game, and Fairlee wasn't getting ahead of him by even an inch. "Am I going to have trouble with you wanting to draw near to me, since you love the smell of roses?"

The smile faded from her face, and she gritted her teeth. "Even roses wouldn't make me want to be close to you."

His grin widened. "I'm hurt that you would be so evil to me."

"You are the wicked one. You wrecked my future."

"No, I didn't. I just kept *you* from wrecking it."

She heard the water sluicing from him when he rose up from the tub, and she couldn't keep her imagination at bay. It was wrong of her to picture him in her mind like that, but she had no control. She put her hands over her eyes, as if that would erase the image, but it didn't.

He pushed the tub outside the door without sloshing out a single drop and laid the wet drying sheets and remaining rose soap beside it. She heard every bit of it and wondered what he wore while he did that chore. Did he have on long underwear like she saw when she helped with the Monday laundry?

She clamped her hands tighter over her

eyes. Only days before, she was going to marry Matthew. It had to be something close to pure old sin for her to envision Isaac in his long underbritches.

"Hey, you can go to bed now," he said softly.

He was so close that his breath was warm on her cheek. She jumped and opened her eyes wide, but by then he'd already jumped into his bed and was under the covers with his head on the pillow. His dark hair had been combed back, leaving furrows where he'd used his fingers rather than a proper comb. He was freshly shaven, and a tiny dot of blood rested on the slight cleft in the center of his chin.

When she found her voice she said, "Well, it's about time. I'd begun to think you were half catfish, the way you stayed in that cold water so long. Or maybe that you'd drowned."

"You wouldn't be so lucky. Seems strange going to bed in the middle of the afternoon, don't it?"

She shrugged one shoulder. "Not to me. I'm exhausted, and it's dark and damp outside. Good night, Isaac."

She crawled into her bed and snuggled down into the feather mattress until she was comfortable. She shut her eyes tightly and willed herself to fall asleep, but it didn't work. When she opened them, he was staring right at her.

"Don't look at me. I'm trying to go to sleep, and it keeps me awake," she said.

"Your sister could demand that I marry you if she found out we'd spent the night in the same room," he said.

"And your brother and cousin? Would they demand that I make an honest man of you?" she asked.

"What do they have to do with anything?" he asked.

"What's good for the goose is good for the gander. If my sister could insist you make an honest woman of me, then why couldn't your relatives insist I make an honest man of you? I'm ruining your reputation too. All I have to do is tell my story honestly, and no woman in Mississippi will want you. So, do we have a deal to be quiet or not?" she asked.

"We have a deal." He flipped over and faced the wall.

She would have never believed a person could actually be too tired to sleep until that moment. She flipped from one side to the other, trying to get comfortable, but she couldn't. She shut her eyes, but all she saw was Isaac's handsome face.

"So, what does your plantation look like? Do you all have separate farms, or is it combined into one big one?" she asked.

He grinned. "Thought we were going to be quiet."

"I can't sleep," she said.

"Me neither. All I could think about for the past two days was a soft bed, and now I can't sleep. Doesn't make a bit of sense. To answer your question, our plantation is one piece of ground. Tyrell's place is on one corner of the property. The old cabin where Dad and Mother started out is diagonally across the land in that corner, and Micah and I have a house pretty close to the middle. We all grew up there together, so we're used to sharing the burden of the jobs as well as the land," he answered.

"Is Delia happy?"

"Very much so. She and Tyrell are still as much in love as they were when they got married. And with a new baby on the way, they truly walk around in the clouds most of the time. It's good to see Tyrell so happy."

"He did seem to be the most serious outlaw among you," she commented.

"He's the oldest and probably thinks deeper than any of us," Isaac agreed with a yawn.

"Think you could sleep now?" she asked.

"Maybe, but I can talk longer if you want."

"I'm glad Delia is happy. She deserves it. She was the strongest one of us and always felt that she had to help raise me and Tempie, even though she's only a year older than I am." She covered a yawn with the back of her hand.

"Sounds like we probably can sleep now," Isaac said. "Good night, Fairlee."

"Good night." She shut her eyes and went right to sleep.

The next morning they were both startled awake by heavy pounding on the door. Isaac sat straight up in the strange room and frowned. Where was he, and how had he gotten there, and who the devil was the woman in the next bed? Reality rushed over him like floodwater as he remembered. He yelled, "Who is it?"

"Etienne. The stage is here. When the horses are done and the drivers have breakfast, they will leave. If you want to be on it, you'd better get around!" he yelled through the wooden door.

"Thank you, sir. We'll be right out," Isaac called back.

"Get up, Fairlee. We've overslept, and we have to be ready to go in short order," he said.

She burrowed down deeper into the soft

mattress and mumbled, "Go away."

He reached across the bed and shook her. "Hey, lady. I'm not Tempie or Delia. Either get up, or get left."

"Go away," she repeated.

Isaac always awoke fully alert and ready to face the day. He slipped into his pants and shirt and grinned. It was payback time for that cold-water stunt the night before. He eased into bed with her and molded his body around her back. "Should we stay in bed all day, or do you want to catch that stage to Monroe?"

The first few words opened her eyes. The rest of the bizarre sentence set her straight up in bed, her long black hair flowing down her back and tickling Isaac's nose.

"We didn't . . . you didn't . . . what happened?"

He rolled off the bed and laughed until his sides ached. "Wake up, Fairlee. We've overslept, and the stagecoach is already here. We'll barely have time for breakfast before we have to leave."

"I slept all afternoon and night?" she asked.

"You did. I'm dressed. I'll go on out and get our food ordered up while you dress and redo your trunk. Come out when you're ready. Unless . . ." He waggled his eyebrows and left the sentence hanging.

"Humph! I'm not that kind of woman. Get out of here. I want ham and eggs and grits. Why did you get into my bed anyway?"

"You wouldn't wake up, and it was payback for the rose-scented cold bath. We are now even," he told her.

"Not by a long shot, mister. You'd better watch your back. You just drew a line in the dirt and challenged a Lavalle. I'll make you pay."

CHAPTER FIVE

Snowflakes floated lazily down from the gray skies, as if they were in no hurry to land. An occasional slight breeze swirled them around like graceful ballerinas on a stage. Then the wind would go completely still, and the flakes would linger between earth and heaven, prolonging their journey to the ground.

Several landed on Fairlee's face when she and Isaac rushed out from the warmth of the station to the stage. She flipped her hood up and barely nodded at the short, round coach driver who waited beside the steps for them. As soon as they were in the coach, he picked up the steps and handed them up to his shotgun rider.

Two men were already in the stage, one on each side. They both looked up when Fairlee put a foot on the wooden step, and one moved over to the other side.

"Thank you," she said, even though she

wasn't totally sure that she might not have liked to sit beside either of the strangers rather than Isaac. The emotions that he'd sent into a tailspin had her mind in a jumble. She'd been in love with Matthew only a few days before, so it had to be wrong to get the jitters every time her fingertips touched Isaac. Besides, she was still angry at him for kidnapping her.

She and Isaac settled into the seat, and she wrapped her cloak tightly around her. It was for warmth but also for protection against his thigh touching her when the coach bumped along the rutted path as it had the day before. The men across from them were smiling at her when she looked up. One was fair-haired, dressed in fine style with a cloak of gray wool and shined boots. The other was his opposite, with dark, brooding looks, but also dressed impeccably, in all black without a hint of road dust or a bit of lint on him. His dark brown eyes felt as if they were burning holes in Fairlee's soul as he scanned her from her toes to the top of her hood. His grin was rakish when he finished his appraisal. She was glad that Isaac had been busy settling in, or he might have said something to the man, and there would have been trouble. She pretended not to even notice his rudeness in assessing her the way he would horseflesh.

"Where are you going?" He shifted his gaze to Isaac.

"We're on our way home to Greenville, Mississippi," Isaac answered.

"We're going home to Monroe. I don't envy you a longer trip at this time of year. I'm Pierre Chamau, and this is my cousin, Claud Yardel. This is a godforsaken mode of travel, isn't it? But it's the way we went, so we don't have horses; therefore, we are at the mercy of this horrid conveyance. Where are you coming from?"

"From Natchitoches," Isaac lied. "We have only been married a short while, and we're on our way home. We'll only be staying a day or so in Monroe before we go on."

"I suppose that is your horse tied behind the stage?" Pierre asked.

"It is," Isaac answered. "How about you? Where are you coming from?"

"Over around Bennet's Bluff. We were visiting a friend," Claud said. His voice was deep with a slight French accent that didn't match his Northern European fair looks.

Isaac felt Fairlee tense. "That truly is a long distance to travel for a visit at this time of year." He nodded.

Claud laughed. "It was much more than a

visit. We were there to support our friend at his wedding. It was meant to be a grand celebration."

Fairlee raised an eyebrow. "Oh?"

They couldn't be talking about Matthew. Their wedding was to be a very small affair, with family only, because her father had been dead but a few months.

"Yes, it was. A very simple wedding but a grand celebration. Finally our friend would be solvent again. His money problems would be over, and he could repay the gambling debts he owes us," Claud said.

" 'Was'? Does that mean the poor fellow had a change of heart, or that he died?" Fairlee asked.

Pierre sighed. "He's very much alive. He's a lucky rogue in that respect. He won't have a nagging woman telling him he can't do this or that and whining at him to stay home with her. From what he told us, she was a fetching little thing with dark hair and blue eyes, somewhat like you have. He was quite excited about having her to squire around on his arm to the winter parties in that part of the world, such as they are in a remote area like that. But rest assured, even if she was pretty, he would have never put up with the whining. The sad side of the coin is that he's still broke."

"So he had a change of heart, did he? Even if she was fetching, he changed his mind?" Fairlee asked.

Claud fluttered his hands in the air. "Not him. The bride. The night before the wedding, she wrote him a note and eloped with another man. Poor old Matthew. There went six months of charm tossed into the river. He was quite despondent about the money. Now he'll have to start all over again."

Isaac covered his gasp with a fake cough.

Fairlee looked at the men innocently and said, "Entertain us with the story. It's a long day in a coach without conversation."

She would rather Isaac wasn't sitting there when she heard the absolute truth, but she couldn't stop herself from asking. She didn't know of another Matthew around her part of the world who'd been about to wed. If the story shaped up the way Isaac and Tempie said it would, she had a right to know. And if it did, she didn't know if she could ever trust another man. Not even someone as honest as Isaac Burnet.

Claud nodded. "Yes, ma'am, the day is forever in one of these contraptions, isn't it? They say we can go twenty miles in eight hours. That gets us from one station stop to the next. They change the horses that often, but sometimes, if there's no room, we have to keep riding. It's not human, I tell you. I told Pierre we were idiots to travel that far in the winter just to get our money back, but Cheval assured him in a letter that he would repay us within a day of marrying the woman."

"It's like traveling in that ark in the Bible that my grandmother read to me," Pierre said. "Had I realized that it would take so long to go, only to be returning home empty-handed, I might even have forgiven Cheval his debt."

"But you wouldn't have gambled with him again, would you?" Claud asked.

"I'm afraid that man has gambled his last in Monroe," Pierre said with a sigh. "His debtors are many, and even though the bride was supposed to have brought enough money to cover them, plus do some minimal repair on that rambling oldhouse that's falling down around his ears. . . . Still, Natchitoches is a different matter. He doesn't owe any debts yet in that part of the world the way he does in Monroe. We can still have good times there winning money off of him. And Matthew always draws the women to him like flies to honey."

Fairlee's lower lip trembled.

Isaac tried to change the subject. "How long have you lived in Monroe?"

"All our lives. But enough about that. The lady asked for a story. I'm not sure it's fit for a lady's ears, but we'll try to make it presentable," Pierre said.

"You just like the sound of your own voice," Claud observed.

"That I do. And it passes the time better than listening to the sound of yours," Pierre told Claud.

Claud chuckled. "Forgive us. We were born the same year twenty-eight years ago, and we've always been more like squabbling siblings than cousins. Pierre is a better storyteller than I am. He can tell you how we came to be riding in Noah's bouncing ark today, rather than getting dressed for a Christmas ball where pretty young ladies await our attention."

Pierre nodded and smiled. "Thank you, Claud. You tell a good tale yourself when you're in the mood. We'll tell our story about why we're in this coach, but if it doesn't fill the hours, then you two must tell yours — about how you met. It's a long way, also, from Mississippi to Natchitoches, Louisiana."

"It's a deal," Fairlee said. Their stupid jaws would come unhinged, and they'd have splinters in their chins if they heard that she was the gullible bride who'd run out on

123

their friend.

"Okay, it all started when we were barely twenty. We met Matthew Cheval at a place where young ladies do not go — a gambling hall on the docks in Natchitoches. If you're from there, you know exactly the kind of place I mean. He was impulsive and fun, and we three became fast friends. For five years we have met there in the spring for a few weeks of debauchery, and he always returns home with us for a few days of gambling in Monroe."

Isaac raised an eyebrow. "Do be careful, sir. You are speaking in front of a lady." His heart went out to Fairlee. She'd been walking on clouds, and now she was being slung to the earth at breakneck speed. She had no choice but to crash. Fairlee was not a whimpering woman, but even a strong woman would have trouble coping with what she was hearing.

Pierre nodded and smiled. " 'Gambling' is a very mild word, sir, for what Matthew had set up for us when we came to Natchitoches. In the beginning he won, but then his luck ran out, and he had to rely on his charm. Lately that's been in slim supply also, so Claud and I have been helping him through the rough spots. It would have done him good to have a wife, but I'm afraid it might not have done her as much good. She was probably wise to elope with the poor dirt farmer she'd met on a trip from Texas last year. Frankly, I don't know why Matthew would want a woman with such a questionable reputation."

Fairlee stifled a gasp. "And did your friend like Natchitoches? It has such lovely places. I loved my time there," she said innocently.

"We all did. It was a free place where few rules applied," Claud said. "You know, this story might be better told and appreciated later over a bottle of wine with only your husband, ma'am. It appears the only way to tell it would be offensive to a lady's tender ears."

Fairlee clenched her teeth. "Then tell me about the bride. Was your friend devastated that the love of his life had left him?"

Claud poked Pierre in the arm. "Ah, the romantic side of Matthew is what she wants to know about."

"The ladies all love him. He's a charmer. What do you think, Claud, is he as good-looking as me?" Pierre teased.

"Yes, my cousin. I hate to tell you this, but the ladies in Natchitoches all declare that he is even better looking than you. They say he dances better and . . ." Claud hesitated. "I won't say more for fear that our

125

new groom will call me out for a duel."

"Did anyone ever call Mr. Cheval out for a duel?" Fairlee asked.

"I could name four or five married men who did. We used to call him the widow-maker," Pierre answered.

"He doesn't sound like a very nice man. Maybe his bride found out about all his dubious escapades?" Fairlee asked.

The coach hit a rut and bounced them around like marbles in a glass jar. Isaac grabbed Fairlee around the waist to keep her from sliding off the bench and onto the floor.

"Easy, darlin'," he said.

"That rut was big enough to bury an elephant in," she mumbled. Her hood had fallen back, and the warmth of his breath on the soft skin of her neck sent shivers down her backbone.

"I swear the ark would be more comfortable, even with having to contend with all those animals," Pierre said.

"The lady asked a question before we all went flopping around like a bunch of drunks on the docks," Claud said.

Pierre raised a dark eyebrow. "Ah, yes, she did. Why are you so interested in our friend?"

"Conversation passes the time on a boring journey. It's a fascinating story, and I'd like to know more about the bride," she said.

Claud laughed again. "Besides, Pierre, you are a gossip worse than an old woman."

Pierre laughed with him. "It does help make the minutes go by faster. Okay, your question was whether he was devastated and the bride justified. In my opinion the answers are no and yes. No, he was not devastated. He was let down because she was bringing a big dowry into the marriage, as I said. Other than that, he didn't really care if he was married or not. A wife will not change Matthew. He'll always do as he pleases. And was she justified? If she'd known that he was marrying her for money, then yes. If she didn't, she was as stupid as he'd declared she was."

Again Fairlee stifled a gasp of outrage. "He said that about his bride? Did you ever meet her? Was she stupid?" Fairlee asked.

"I'd never say that about *you*," Isaac said.

"You'd better not. I can shoot better than you can run," she said flatly.

"Aha! You've married a woman who will make you toe the line. Matthew needs a woman like that, but I'm afraid if and when he marries, he will keep her very firmly under his thumb," Pierre said.

"I'm afraid I have married a willful

woman, but I knew what I was getting when I proposed. Perhaps Matthew should marry such a lady. She might settle him down once and for all." Isaac grinned.

Pierre reassessed Fairlee with her black hair and blue eyes. "Matthew said his bride was a wallflower. He'd tried to marry her older sister last spring but was too late. He said if this sister didn't work out, there was one more in the litter he could charm. But we never met any of the women. I'm not sure we would have even if the wedding had come off without a hitch. The next morning we had plans to catch a boat down to Natchitoches for a week to celebrate."

A smile tickled Fairlee's mouth. " 'Litter'? And why would he be going to gamble when he was supposed to be honeymooning with his wife?"

"That's what he said. Three women in the litter, and he'd wind up with one of them to get the money they'd inherited from their mother. You'd have to know Matthew to understand. A wife might be necessary, but she'll never be the love of his life, ma'am."

Fairlee smiled brightly, thinking about what Matthew would run into if he tried to sweet-talk Tempest. There'd better be someone in Hades making room for another doomed soul, because Tempie would shoot him and make sure no one ever found the body.

"Why would he leave his bride behind and not take her to Natchitoches with him?" Fairlee asked.

Pierre sighed again. The woman was so innocent. "Haven't you been listening? It wasn't a marriage of love. The woman wanted a husband. Matthew wanted her money. They would both be happy."

Fairlee touched her forehead. "Oh, now I see. Well, it sounds as if you two were sorely disappointed. No wedding. No grand celebration in Natchitoches. And now a bumpy ride home."

Claud nodded seriously. "That's the truth."

They rode in silence for a mile or more before Pierre spoke up. "You were going to tell us how you met to finish up the trip."

"It's a very long story," Isaac said.

The coach came to a halt, and Isaac pulled back the leather window covering. Snow was falling so hard that it looked like heavy fog. The driver slung open the door and poked his head inside the coach.

"We're stopping here for the rest of the day and night. There's no way we can get to Monroe until this lets up. There's a small station here. The owner will have food, and he has one room to let. Me and my shotgun rider can stay in the dining room beside the fireplace. You all can fight to the death for the room, for all I care. We ain't makin' another mile until it stops snowing," he said.

"What a mess," Pierre said when he stepped out into the snow.

Claud ducked his head against the blizzard and followed his cousin toward the lights of the house.

"Ready to brave it?" Isaac asked Fairlee.

"Ready as I'll ever be."

"I'm sorry about all that," he said as he helped her from the stage.

"I'm not. Now I know the truth, and I'd rather not talk about it ever again."

He took her arm and led her to the station house. "I understand."

The wind whistled through the bare tree limbs, using them like the strings on a harp. It threw snowflakes against Fairlee's face with such force that they stung like bees. When Isaac pushed open the door, she was more than glad to hurry inside toward the blazing flames in the fireplace.

"We were just telling the good man here that we'd been so engrossed with our conversation that we didn't realize how bad the weather had gotten," Pierre said.

The station owner was a short, round man

130

with a bald head, a bushy black beard, and a jolly expression. "Good afternoon. I've got a good fire going and a nice pot of chicken soup on the stove. Wife made up some bread this morning, so it's fresh. We're out of cheese, but we've got tea and coffee aplenty. Remove your coats and get some warmth into your bones. I expect it's going to be a long, long night."

"I understand you have a room to let?" Isaac said.

"Two rooms. These gentlemen have taken one. Do you and the missus want the other?" he asked.

"Yes, and she will be going up to the room straightaway. Could you bring her food up to her? She's not feeling so well," Isaac said.

"I'm fine, Isaac," she hissed.

Isaac put his hand on Fairlee's back and ushered her toward the stairs. "Shh. It's all right to have your meal in our room. Those headaches come on fast, don't they? Maybe I'll just have my meal with her so she won't be alone. It's been a pleasure meeting you gentlemen, and thank you for the conversation on the stage. Perhaps we'll see you in the morning."

The station manager called out, "Take your pick of the rooms. Both have two beds, and we started up a fire in both rooms when the weather turned bad. Figured we'd have guests. You will pay up before you leave in the morning, won't you?"

"We surely will. Keep a tab of what we owe," Isaac said. "Perhaps an extra pot of tea would be helpful."

"What are you doing?" Fairlee whispered.

"Protecting you. I promised Delia I would deliver you safe and sound."

The staircase was steep and narrow, permitting only one person at a time. He stood to one side and let Fairlee go up ahead of him. Halfway up her boot heel caught in the bottom of her cape, and she faltered. He put a hand on each side of her waist and caught her before she could fall backward, sending both of them hind end over forehead to the bottom of the steps.

"Whoa! Don't faint on me now. Wait until we're in our room, and you can stretch out on a bed," he said loudly enough for the men in the dining room to hear.

"I'm not about to faint. I'm not a weakling. I tripped," she whispered.

"I know that, but they don't," he said.

He opened both doors on the landing. The room to the left had two beds, a washstand with a pitcher of water and a bowl on the top and clean drying towels on the rack, two straight-backed chairs facing the fireplace, and a window that overlooked the front of the station. The other one was identical down to the color of the quilts on the beds but faced the back of the station.

Isaac chose the one on the left.

"Why this one?" she asked.

"I like the look of it better, and I want to see what's going on. My horse is out there," he explained.

"You couldn't see that far if you tried. Your horse could be still tied to the stage and freezing to death."

She untied her cape and hung it over the back of a chair with the wet hem toward the warmth of the fire. Had she been home, she and Tempie would have frolicked in the snow like children. They'd only seen it twice that Fairlee could remember, and they'd had so much fun both times. Of course, Delia had been home, and they'd all been young, so they all romped around in the snow together. And then they'd made ice cream with thick cream and whipped eggs, and Fairlee had almost gotten sick from eating too much.

Isaac pulled back the curtain and looked out at the heavy snow. "I can see shadows, and the man is leading my horse to the barn right now."

In three easy strides she was across the

room, and, sure enough, she could see either the driver or his shotgun rider taking the horse toward the barn, where a yellow glow beckoned to the animals and men alike to come in out of the bad weather. She shivered when she thought about how fortunate they'd been to leave Texas in the spring and not the winter. They'd slept in barns like that one and were glad to be inside out of the rain, but they'd never had to travel through deep snow.

When she turned to say something to Isaac, he was sitting in the empty chair and warming his hands by the fire. "You thinking about how lucky we were not to have to try to forage for food and shelter in this kind of weather last spring?"

She nodded and perched on the edge of the chair where her cape was draped. "Yes, I was. Now, tell me, why are we up here instead of in the dining room until bedtime?"

"It was time for us to tell *our* story. Remember what they said about Cheval telling them his bride had been on a journey from Texas to Louisiana last year? And he told them about his bride being pretty with dark hair and blue eyes? Pierre already looked at you as if he knew something. I'm not sure they aren't already suspicious. If your bridegroom mentioned that we were eloping to Mississippi, they might try something stupid like taking you back to him. We never did tell them our names, and that, too, could come out in the course of an afternoon of conversation. It's easier if you have a headache," he said.

"Stop calling that scoundrel my bridegroom, and those men wouldn't try to take me back now. Matthew wouldn't have me if they did. Besides, they think we're married." Her chin quivered at what a wretch Matthew had turned out to be.

Fairlee's distress didn't escape Isaac's notice, but he decided not to say a word about it and let her have her dignity. "Who cares? It's far better they think we're eager to be alone than for us to make a slip that will prove beyond a doubt the notions they might already be entertaining. Besides, after we eat, I plan on taking another long, long nap. When we get to Monroe and buy you a horse, it'll be at least a week before either of us has an entire night's sleep. Remember the watches?"

Her moan was slight, but it was audible, and she stiffened her chin. "I remember, though I'd hoped to forget them. We'll have to travel with those two the rest of the way to Monroe tomorrow."

Isaac looked over at her. "Maybe not. It shouldn't be that far. I figure we came more than halfway from the last stop, so maybe we'll just sit it out and wait for the next stage to come through. Your headache could linger."

She sank into the depths of his green eyes for a split second before she looked away. He might prove right about her headache. Likely it would linger as long as she had to share time and space with Isaac Burnet, because he was a pain in her neck and head. She was already tired of trying to figure out why she was drawn to the man so much more than she had been to her bridegroom.

Bridegroom, nothing! Had I known what he was really, truly after . . . she thought, and she turned around so Isaac couldn't see the misery in her face.

Her inner voice butted in and began to fuss before she could even finish thinking the sentence. *You were told by the three people you trust the most in the world. Then there were the letters from Delia. And, last, she sent Isaac to beg for her. So don't be saying that you didn't know. You knew, all right. You just didn't want to admit that you had made a big mistake.*

They heard a man swearing under his breath before he kicked the door with the toe of his boot. Isaac was quick to jump up and open it, then reach for the tray that held two large bowls of soup and a loaf of bread.

"Thank you, sir, for this service," Isaac said.

"Navigating those stairs with hot food is a chore. I ain't so sure I can get her trunk up here," he grumbled.

"How about I go back with you and bring up the trunk, then I'll go back for the hot tea?" Isaac offered.

"For that I'll throw in a couple of pieces of the wife's dried-apple cake and not even charge you." The man's countenance changed from sour to smiling.

Fairlee was alone for the first time since she'd been kidnapped when the door shut behind them. If she wanted to, she could open the window, slide off the porch roof onto the ground, steal Isaac's horse, and make her way back to Bennet's Bluff. Going home didn't mean she would marry that scoundrel, Matthew Cheval. It might mean that she and Tempie would take care of him so that no other women would fall under his smooth-talking spell.

Were all men like Matthew?

No, some are trustworthy. Uncle Jonathan is a wonderful man, and so was my father, and even Tyrell from what Delia writes to me. And

as much as I hate to admit it, so is Isaac Bur-
net, even if he is an outlaw.

She laid her warm palm on the window and shuddered. Her life with Matthew would have been as cold as the window even in the summer heat. What if she had brought children into such a loveless marriage? She felt as if she had walked out to the edge of a steep, rocky cliff, about to fall to sudden death with the next step if she had promised to love, honor, and obey a man like Matthew. At least Isaac had saved her from a lifetime of misery, and she owed him for that much.

But she'd never admit that to Isaac or to Delia or even to Tempie.

"You look like you just saw a ghost," Isaac said from the doorway.

She'd been so deep in thought that she hadn't heard him coming up the steps or opening the door. He set a tray with tea and two big pieces of cake on a chair beside their soup and bread. She glanced at both and realized she was hungry. Life went on even when the heart was heavy.

CHAPTER SIX

Monroe was cold, but the roads were clear. They'd left the last station on the midmorning stage going east. The first stage going back west that morning had brought news that they'd only been in the edge of the snowstorm and that if they'd traveled but a short distance, the roads would have been fine. Three miles away from the station they left the snow and ice behind, and the roads were dry all the way into Monroe.

"I feel sorry for that family going west with those small children," Fairlee said when they finally began to go faster.

"Maybe they'll make it to the first station and put up there for the night, and tomorrow the sun will melt part of the snow away. Did you ever travel by stage when you were a little girl?" Isaac said.

"A few times. Mother took us to New Orleans to visit her relatives once a year. Most of the time we took a carriage and a couple of wagons to tote our things."

"How did you entertain yourselves?" he asked.

She smiled, and his heart melted. "We became Indian witches."

"You became what?" he gasped.

"Witches. We put spells on imaginary enemies who were chasing us with intentions of kidnapping us for our magic powers. They were always right outside the carriage. Tempie usually came up with the most ingenious spells. Once she turned them all into wolves and then shot them with our imaginary guns."

"What did your mother think of such talk?"

Fairlee's smile widened, and her eyes glittered. "She was the one who started it. We were whining when we were about six, seven, and eight, and she told us to use our imagination and pretend that we were little Indians who had great powers. After that we played Indian witches all the time. Once we even staked Tempest out on a pile of wood to see if she could escape death by fire, but Mother caught us."

"Good Lord!"

"We wouldn't have really lit the fire. Delia told Tempest to scream and beg for her life, but she wouldn't. She just chanted a curse on the two of us. Mother told us we couldn't play the game anymore."

Isaac shuddered. "Did you stop?"

"No, but we didn't get caught again, and we gave up seeing if a witch could survive fire."

"You were hellions from birth," he said.

"Don't you ever forget it, and we grew up to be even worse hellions. If I ever play witch again and stake you out on a pyre, remember that my mother isn't here to save you," she whispered.

"You'd have never survived Salem," he said.

"I almost didn't survive the Alamo."

"Had you stayed, the Alamo might not have survived you."

She laughed. "You got that right, Mr. Burnet."

It was past noon when the stage stopped in downtown Monroe, a prominent trading center with a hotel, general store, and a blacksmith. Fairlee was never so glad to see civilization in her life. She wanted to prowl through the general store first, but Isaac insisted on making sure they had rooms for the night.

He led her to the hotel first and booked two rooms with an adjoining door for one night. Then they sat down at a table beside the fireplace and ordered a midafternoon meal of roast pork, potatoes and carrots, steamed cabbage, and fresh hot cornbread. She could hardly eat for looking out the window at the stores across the street.

"You'd better eat better than that. It's a week to Greenville, and we'll be living on whatever we can shoot or trap," Isaac said.

"Do I get a gun?" she asked.

He didn't answer.

She raised her voice. "Did you hear me?"

"I did, and I'm thinking about it. Will you give me your word you won't shoot me or wait until I'm asleep and take off back to Bennet's Bluff?"

"You'd believe me if I gave you my word? What if I was lying?"

He broke off a piece of cornbread and covered it with fresh-cream butter before popping it into his mouth. "Lavalles are stubborn, hardheaded, and sometimes as mean as rattlesnakes, but they are honest. If you give your word, you'll stand by it."

"I give you my word," she said.

"Then you can have a gun."

"I'll also need a bow and a quiver of arrows and a knife. I'll pick them all out myself as well as my horse and saddle. Tempie packed trousers and shirts for me, so I'll be changing into them and packing my saddlebags. My trunk will have to be left behind. Maybe we can trade it for part of the hotel rent."

Isaac chuckled.

"What's so amusing?" she asked.

"You. A week ago you were ready to go home to Cheval. Now you sound eager to be on your way to Delia," he answered.

"A blink of the eye can change things, Mr. Burnet. We were all set to live in Texas until Father finished his assignment there, but one morning at breakfast he announced that we were leaving in half an hour and that we were nuns. What about that poor woman we found dead with her baby still in her arms? Do you think she knew that morning that she'd never live to see the sunset or that her precious daughter would be raised by strangers? Yes, a week has changed me. I am eager to get to Delia's, but I'm not angry at her anymore. She and Tempie could see what I couldn't. Maybe someday I'll be able to return the favor. Now finish your meal. We have shopping to do."

Isaac was stunned. He'd known the Lavalle women were strong, but he never knew just how much inner strength they had, and at that moment he admired Fairlee more than he ever had in the past.

"Don't look at me like that. If you're waiting for weeping and gnashing of teeth so you can comfort me, you've got quite a wait in store. You'll have a long gray beard and be getting around with a cane before that happens. Yes, I'm mad at Matthew for using me like that, and I hope that someday he does marry for money — and gets a woman who makes him earn every single penny of it."

Isaac laughed.

"It's not funny."

"I didn't say it was. Cheval deserves to be shot. Maybe one of these days he won't be the widow-maker. Maybe a cuckolded husband will take care of him," Isaac said.

"Oh, no, that's much too easy. He deserves to live a long, long life and be miserable every day of it."

"Whew! The tone in your voice tells me I don't want you mad at *me*," he said.

"What makes you think I've forgiven you for kidnapping me?"

"You are a hard woman, Fairlee."

"Don't forget it."

They finished their meal in silence, and both stood up at the same time. She pulled her cape tightly around her shoulders, and he shoved his arms down into the sleeves of his coat. She started toward the door, and he followed.

When they were outside on the wooden sidewalk, he pointed toward the stables, and she nodded, even though she itched to get inside that general store. Horse first, supplies next.

There were two horses for sale at the livery. One was a roan with a white piebald face, the other a big black beast that rivaled Isaac's prize animal for size.

A man approached them from a room in the back. "Y'all interested in buyin', or are you just lookin'?"

"I'm Isaac Burnet, and this is my wife, Fairlee. The horse that the stagecoach driver brought in for the night is mine. My wife needs one too," he said.

"Pleased to make your acquaintance. I'm Jerome Wiltz. Owned this and the black-smith shop for nigh on to ten years now. Hamp said that a man by your name would come to claim his horse in the morning. You lookin' for something to ride or a pack animal?"

"Both," Fairlee said.

"Well, I got a mule that's pretty sturdy. I reckon it would carry your supplies. But I only got these two horses for sale. How long y'all goin' to be on the road? Bad time of year to be travelin' like that." He spit a stream of brown tobacco juice onto the straw-covered floor.

"I like the black one," Fairlee said.

"That ain't no horse for a woman. The roan is a better choice. She's a good mare, easy to get along with. That old boy is meaner'n a hungry mountain lion. A woman couldn't control him," Jerome said.

"You saddle him, and I'll be back in exactly fifteen minutes. If he throws me, I'll take the roan," she told the blacksmith.

Jerome's eyes widened. "Is she serious?"

"I'm afraid she is. She can ride anything that has four legs," Isaac said.

"I won't be responsible for her death if he throws her off and stomps her."

"Trust me, he won't," Isaac told him.

"I've only got one sidesaddle, and I'm not sure it'll fit him. I bought it with the roan. She's used to it. You sure you won't change your mind, ma'am?"

Fairlee pointed toward a row of saddles. "Any one of those is fine. I do not ride sidesaddle."

The men had barely finished cinching the saddle when she reappeared in the stable. She whipped back her cape, stepped up into the stirrups, and threw a leg over the animal. She flipped her cape over his haunches and reined him back. She leaned forward and whispered into his ear, petting his head the whole time.

"We are going to get along just fine. It's a long ride to Delia's, and if you take me there, I promise you pastures of green grass and exercise every day. If you buck me off or give me a minute's trouble, I will shoot you and pay the man to haul your carcass away," she said.

Jerome rubbed his scraggly beard. "I'll be danged. I woulda swore he'd throw him a fit when he smelled a woman on his back. Don't seem fittin' for a lady to wear them kind of clothes or to ride a big stallion like him."

"I don't care what seems 'fittin' to you or any other man," Fairlee said. "I'm going to ride down the street to make sure this cape doesn't spook him. If he acts right, I will buy him and the saddle."

Jerome scratched his head. "You didn't ask me how much I was chargin' for him."

"I know what he's worth, and you won't overcharge me."

She touched the stallion with her knee, and he turned around and trotted off down the street, prancing high. When she slapped him on the back end, he speeded up, but he didn't flinch when the cape flopped onto his back.

"Well?" Jerome asked, when she rode him

back into the stable.

"I like him. We do well together. Is he gun-shy?"

"Nope. I bought him last week from a feller come through here from back east. Said he was tired of ridin' a horse and ready for a stagecoach to take him on to somewhere in the west. He's a spirited thing, but he ain't gun-shy," Jerome said.

"I will give you five dollars for him and the saddle," she said.

Jerome rubbed his beard again.

Fairlee wanted to tell him that rubbing it wouldn't make him any smarter, but she held her tongue and waited.

"I paid that for him and the saddle, and I've fed and housed him for a week. I was thinking more like eight," Jerome finally said.

"Seven," Fairlee said.

"Seven-fifty, and we'll be even on his keep until morning." Jerome stuck out his hand.

She shook it and pulled a small drawstring purse from inside her cape. She counted out seven bills and several coins to make up the exact amount. "Don't be switching saddles. I like this one."

"Wouldn't dream of it. That's the one that was on his back when I bought him, so he's used to it." Jerome shoved the money into his pocket. "Want to see the mule? I've got four that I bought off a man passing through who decided to stay right here in Monroe. His wife and kids were sick to death of traveling in a covered wagon."

Fairlee nodded and followed the men to the back of the barn. She picked out the best of the four mules and gave Jerome two dollars and fifty cents for the animal.

"Sure you don't want to buy two of them?" Jerome asked.

"No, one is plenty," Fairlee said. "Now let's go get our supplies. The stores will all close at dusk, and the sun is setting."

"Bet she don't whine, does she?" Jerome smiled.

"Never known her to," Isaac said.

"Any more where she come from?"

"One, but she's even more stubborn than that one," Isaac said.

"I'm standing right here," Fairlee said loudly.

Jerome ignored her comment. "Pretty as that one?"

"Naw, but she ain't ugly." Isaac grinned.

Fairlee fought back a blush. No one had ever thought she was as pretty as, let alone prettier than, Tempie. Delia was elegantly beautiful with her straight black hair and crystal-clear blue eyes. Words couldn't

149

describe Tempest Lavalle. She had curly hair that lay in natural ringlets and smoky blue eyes. She was more than a pretty face — more like a force of nature. When she walked into a room, men stopped in mid-sentence to stare at her, and women envied her.

"Well, you ever get a chance, you toss her over the fence into Monroe and tell her to come visitin' old Jerome Wiltz. I'd treat her right if she's that pretty and can ride as good as your woman," Jerome said.

Your woman! The two words stuck in Fairlee's mind, and she couldn't shake them loose. She wasn't anyone's woman.

"If I ever see her again, I'll tell her. Good day to you, Mr. Wiltz. We'll see you in the morning to square up our bill. I expect it'll be pretty early," Isaac said.

"I'm up long before the crack of dawn," he said as he waved them away.

Women nodded and smiled at Fairlee on the way down the street to the general store. At least until they noticed that she was wearing trousers under her cape, and then they looked as if they'd been sucking lemons. The lady in the store gasped at Fairlee's appearance.

Fairlee held her head high as she headed toward the counter at the back. "We're here to buy supplies for a weeklong ride."

"Flour, salt, bacon?" the woman asked even as she frowned.

"I've got two cups, a coffeepot, two plates, and two forks in my travel kit," Isaac said.

Fairlee nodded. "Then we'll need coffee to start with and a jar of bacon drippings if you've got it," she told the shopkeeper.

The woman started a list on a scrap of paper. "Just rendered out a hog last week. It's still fresh."

"Milk?" Fairlee asked.

"I could fix you up with a quart of buttermilk that would keep a couple of days, but it'll be in a jar."

"We'll pack it gently," Fairlee said. "Small bit of baking soda and two onions. Maybe a little bag of potatoes."

"Maybe we should have bought the second mule," Isaac said.

"You want to starve?" Fairlee asked.

"Y'all ain't been married long, have you?" The woman finally smiled.

"No, ma'am, we have not," Fairlee said.

"It shows. Mister, one mule can carry enough supplies for a week. You must be goin' north. If you was goin' any other way, you'd be takin' the stage. Want me to add some sugar?"

Fairlee nodded. "And a quarter pound of tea."

"That'll be four dollars and a dime."

Fairlee looked at Isaac. "Pay the woman."

"I thought you were taking care of this," he said.

"I wouldn't be here if it weren't for you, so you get to pay." Poisoned honey dripped from her tone.

"You paid for the horse," he argued.

"Yes, I did, and it's my horse, and I'll keep it when we get to Mississippi. This is food for the trip, and that's, clearly, your responsibility," Fairlee said.

Isaac pulled bills from his coat pocket and handed them to the woman. "Add a bottle of whiskey to that order, and keep the change."

"Why?" Fairlee asked.

"I'll need it to spend a week with you on the trail," he smarted off.

Fairlee pulled a handful of coins from her reticule and pushed them across the counter. "Make that two bottles of whiskey."

CHAPTER SEVEN

Fairlee went through her trunk, tossing everything onto the bed. Two work dresses, two pairs of trousers, and three shirts. One coat for riding, similar to the one Isaac wore. Fairlee figured she could wear the cape over it if it got very cold. She'd made up her mind that she wouldn't leave the garment behind. They'd trapped and tanned too many rabbits for the fur, and they'd shared in the sewing, so it was going with her to Delia's.

She finally settled on the trousers and shirts, one dress, and undergarments. That was enough to get her through a week, and then she and Delia could either make new clothes or else bring in a seamstress for a few weeks.

"As if it will matter what I look like anyway," she muttered as she repacked the trunk. The hotel owner had offered them the price of their rooms for the chest and whatever Fairlee left inside it. He was getting a good deal. Her dresses and cotton nightgown were worth more than that.

She sat on the edge of the bed and sipped the lukewarm tea she'd had delivered earlier. If only she'd gone with Tyrell and Delia eight months before, she wouldn't be in this mess. She and Tempie should have both already been in Mississippi. But Tempie had wanted to visit their cousins in southern Louisiana, and Fairlee had been in a big hurry to get on with her wedding plans.

"I shall never do anything in a hurry again. *Wait* and *patience* are my two new words," she said to herself.

She finished the tea and put on the soft white cotton nightgown one more time. For the next week she'd sleep in her pants and shirt with the cape pulled up around her like a blanket, probably on the cold ground or, if they were lucky, in an abandoned barn. She ran a hand down the front of the gown and sighed. She'd miss crawling into a bed, even if Isaac was snoring in the one next to her.

She went to the door and pressed her ear against it, but she couldn't hear his snores, so he had to be making his own preparations for the trip. She wouldn't even admit it to God, much less to Isaac, but she missed his presence. Even if they did fight like two territorial yard cats, she suddenly hated being alone.

Isaac unpacked and repacked his saddlebags. Some of the things could be loaded onto the mule, giving him more room for ammunition. The whole job took less than ten minutes. He flopped down onto the bed and stared at the door, trying to will it to open — or, better yet, disappear entirely, making his room and Fairlee's adjoining chamber one. He missed Fairlee and didn't fully trust her to stay put when he wasn't right there beside her. He inhaled deeply and let it out slowly. If she ran, she'd better not stop, because he wouldn't quit chasing her until he had her back in his clutches.

"I promised Delia, and I will deliver her," he whispered to the door.

He had to admit that it was more than that, though. He wanted to show Fairlee that he was just as persistent and strong-willed as she was. She'd fascinated him from the beginning of their days together in Texas. To his way of thinking, she was the prettiest and the strongest of the Lavalle women. Probably because she was the middle child, much like he was.

In reality, he was the older of the two Burnet brothers, but they'd been raised right alongside their cousin Tyrell, who was five years older than Isaac and far more like a brother than a cousin. That had meant that for years he and Fairlee were never old enough to do what the elder sibling did yet too old to be babied, and thus they'd had to forge their own way.

She'd taken the kidnapping better than he'd thought she would, or else she was a very good actress. Even when the men in the stagecoach had talked about the wedding and how Matthew Cheval hadn't been overly upset by Fairlee's running away, she'd kept a stiff upper lip. She was a woman any man would be proud to ride the river with.

But that man had best get ready for a bumpy ride, because Fairlee was a ball of fire, and it would take a man willing to walk beside her, not ahead of her. Finally he pushed himself up from the bed and padded to the door in his stocking feet. He pressed his ear against the wood, but Fairlee must have already been asleep, because he couldn't hear a thing going on in the next room.

He tiptoed back to the bed and stretched out, lacing his hands behind his head. To make it home in a week, they'd need to do twenty miles each day. He'd done far more than that when he was riding hell-bent for western Louisiana to talk her out of marrying Cheval, and it had been a dang good thing. One lazy day on the trip and he'd have been too late. He shuddered at the thought of Fairlee's making a lifetime commitment to someone as despicable as Cheval.

His eyes grew heavy, and he blew out the lamp sitting on the washstand at the end of the bed. He could see a soft yellow glow under the door. Surely Fairlee hadn't gone to sleep with the lamp still burning. He got up and went to knock gently on the door.

"Come in," she said.

She was sitting in front of the window with the curtain pulled back slightly so she could see the street below.

"What do you need?" she asked without turning her head.

He swallowed twice before he could speak. She was so beautiful, with her dark hair flowing down her back to almost brush the floor. He longed to run his fingers through it to see if it was as silky as it looked. The soft glow from the lamp and what moonlight filtered into the room cast her face into shadow on one side and brightness on the other. Had an artist painted her exactly like that, he could have sold the painting for a king's ransom.

"I thought you'd fallen asleep with the lamp on, and I was going to blow it out for you," he said.

"Go ahead. I should be in bed already. We will have to be up very early to make good time tomorrow," she said.

When she wasn't snapping at him, her voice was like a shot of good, smooth whiskey with just a few drops of pure, fresh honey to cut the bite.

"Breakfast is served at six o'clock. Will you be ready then?" he asked.

She still didn't look back at him. "Long before that."

"Then good night, Fairlee," he said.

"Isaac, will you please leave the door open?" It took all the willpower she could conjure up to ask, but the reason she hadn't gone to bed was because she didn't want to be alone in the strange room.

"Of course," he said.

He blew out the lamp, left the door open, and they both slept that deep, undisturbed rest largely reserved for children who've played hard all day long.

When Fairlee awoke, she could hear Isaac in the other room sloshing water as he shaved and got ready for the next leg of their journey.

She shut the door and unbuttoned her nightgown. When she was fully dressed, she folded the garment and placed it in the trunk. She wondered what lady would wear it next. A new mother who needed extra lying-in gowns? Or perhaps a woman who'd been kidnapped and didn't have a sister to pack her things?

When she cracked the door open, Isaac was sitting in his chair beside the window. "Looks like it could be a clear day. Today is the first day of the New Year. Did you realize that?"

"I didn't. Are you ready to grab a quick breakfast and be on the road?"

"Are you?" he asked.

She shoved a long, slender knife into the sheath on the outside of her boot. "I wish it was done and I was already there."

Her rifle would fit into the sheath on the saddle, and she'd ride with the quiver of arrows on her back and the bow hung on the saddle, where she could reach it quickly. Yes, Fairlee was ready for everything but the turmoil in her heart and soul.

They ate ham and eggs, hot biscuits and grits for breakfast and asked the cook to pack them a sack of biscuits stuffed with

159

ham for their noon meal. When they rode out of town with the mule behind Isaac, the sun was peeking over the eastern horizon off to their right, pushing its way up behind bare-limbed trees to a glorious new day.

Monroe, with its early-morning sounds, quickly faded into the background and was replaced by a lonesome coyote howling about having to get up so early. Fairlee could relate to it. She'd wanted to snuggle down into the covers that morning. Had she been at home on the plantation, she might have asked for a tray to be brought to her room so she didn't have to dress until mid-morning. But if she'd been at home, she wouldn't have been in her childhood bed. She would have awakened in her marriage bed — without a husband. He would have been in Natchitoches with his friends, carousing for women to make widows of and gambling away her money as if it grew on trees.

"You sure are quiet this morning," Isaac said.

"So are you," she countered.

"Want to talk about him?"

"Who?"

"Cheval?"

"No. What's done is done. Apparently God watches over fools and idiots."

"I don't think you are a fool or an idiot, Fairlee Lavalle," he said.

"Of course I'm not. Matthew Cheval is both. He should have already been shot for philandering or gambling, but there he is, still alive, the lying scoundrel."

"I don't think God has anything to do with that. Cheval's luck will play out one of these days. I'm glad you escaped him. Delia kept saying he was horrid, but I had no idea he was that despicable," Isaac said.

"It's in the past. Leave it there," she said bluntly.

He changed the subject. "This seems familiar, doesn't it?"

"Seems like we did ride side by side quite often on our trip from Texas. Do you think this one will be as eventful?" she asked.

"I hope not!" he exclaimed. "I'd just as soon get you to Delia and Tyrell's place and get on home to my own life."

"Got someone waiting for you there?"

"Micah."

"You know what I mean. Is there a wife or the promise of one?" She held her breath.

"No wife. No promise. Micah has been interested in a woman, but not me. I'm going to be the old bachelor uncle all the kids love. I'm going to carve whistles for them and teach them to ride and shoot," he said.

161

She smiled. "You like kids?"

"Adore them. I can't wait for Delia and Tyrell's firstborn to arrive. Delia will have to hurry up and have another one or two, or else this one will be so spoiled, no one will be able to stand it." Isaac's voice sounded happy when he talked about the new baby.

"Well, I intend to do my very best to add to that spoiling. Tempie said she'd be there by the time the baby comes. Aunt Rachel is sending her with an escort so she can bring our cradle from the attic. She's been sewing tiny clothes for months now. Poor Delia will be overwhelmed when Tempie arrives."

"To have all three of you sisters together when the baby gets there should make Delia happy," Isaac said.

"You like Delia a lot, don't you?"

"I'd have to like her a lot to be on this trip with you, wouldn't I?"

"That was pretty blunt."

"I'm honest."

She shot a mean look his way. "Yes, you are. And that's the reason you'll be the cranky old uncle instead of a loving father."

"Well, pardon me for speaking my mind."

She smiled. "I guess both of us are prone to do that, aren't we?"

"Yes, we are," he agreed.

Deep in their own thoughts, they rode side by side the rest of the morning. At noon they stopped beside a clear creek and had their meal of biscuits and ham while the horses and mule tugged at a few blades of grass and drank the water. They rested no more than half an hour before settling back into their saddles and heading on north.

The afternoon wore on and on, and Fairlee shifted her weight from the left hip to the right. Finally she stopped trying to get comfortable and endured the ache in both hips until the sun began to set. They passed several homesteads with smoke spiraling from the chimneys, and she longed to knock on the door and beg for a place on the floor to sleep for the night.

"Are you going to push me to ride all night?" he finally asked.

"I'm not pushing you. I've been ready to stop for an hour, but I wasn't about to admit it, or you'd say I was whining," she answered.

"Well, I see an old barn up ahead. Looks like the house burned. I don't reckon they'd mind if we holed up inside the barn." He turned his face so she couldn't see his grin.

"I could sleep standing up in a broom closet. If you'll take care of the horses, I'll start a fire and fry some bacon and a few

163

potatoes for our supper," she said.

His grin widened. "You shirkin' your duties with the horses?"

"You kidnapped me, remember? I didn't ask to be hauled away from my warm bed in the middle of winter, and I dang sure didn't ask to ride twenty miles a day in a bumpy old stagecoach or on the back of a horse. If I sat down and whined and carried on like an overindulged child, you wouldn't have a leg to stand on in an argument. So you can take care of the horses. At least I'm nice enough to offer to cook supper."

"Delia is going to owe me for the rest of her life. And I didn't kidnap you, darlin', I rescued you."

"Don't call me darlin', and you did not 'rescue' me. You kidnapped me. But right now I'm hungry, so it doesn't much matter how I got here. What matters is that I get supper ready." She slid off the horse and eyed the barn. She could see hay in the loft, so the horses and mule would be fed.

"There's an old stone well. If it's got water, we're in luck. Want me to draw up enough so you can take a bath?" he teased.

She pointed a long, slender finger at him. "When I'm tired, I get mean. When I'm hungry, I get cranky. When I'm saddle sore, I get real ugly. I'm all three right now. You sure you want to tease me?"

"I like my bacon rendered out until it's crispy, and I like onions in my potatoes," he said, shrugging.

"I like my horse rubbed down and well fed."

She followed the mule to the back of the barn to what was left of a stable. Boards were loose, but if they tied the animal, it should stay until morning. A cat slithered out from behind a mound of hay while Fairlee was unpacking the things they'd need for cooking, and she sighed in relief. She hated rats, and they often found refuge in a barn. Hopefully, the cat had already taken care of all the rats in that particular barn.

She started a fire out beside the well and set up her skillet.

Soon bacon was sizzling, the aroma wafting inside to Isaac. His stomach growled in anticipation. Then he caught a whiff of onions frying, and he really got hungry.

Hungry, tired, and saddle sore — Fairlee's assessment of her condition described him to a tee also. Only difference was, he didn't get mean, cranky, or ugly. He got sleepy. And he'd have to take the first watch. He couldn't leave Fairlee unprotected all night, not in strange country.

"You plannin' on takin' first watch?" she asked a few minutes later, as if reading his mind.

They ate standing up, using the well cover for a table.

"Thought I would," he said.

"I've got a better idea," she said.

"Why does that surprise me?"

"Don't get snippy with me, Isaac. The loft has a ladder that can be pulled up. There is no way anyone could get up there without our hearing them. We could both sleep at the same time."

"And the horses? Reckon we could make the mule and the horses climb up there with us? If someone was out to do some stealing, he'd think he'd run onto a gold mine with those two horses and all the supplies."

"Hell's bells!"

"Fairlee! Ladies don't use words like that."

"Right now I don't give a hoot. I'm tired, and I want to sleep."

He pointed to the ladder. "Go sleep. I'll keep the fire going and clean up the mess. I'll wake you for the second shift. That way you can cook breakfast like Delia did on the Texas trip. I'll catch four hours of good sleep, and we'll eat and be on our way before sunup."

She didn't argue, which surprised him.

"Thank you."

"You won't be thanking me when I wake you up for your watch. By noon you'll be sleeping in the saddle."

She didn't answer. There wasn't any need, because he was right, as much as it aggravated her to admit it. She put a boot on the first rung and started up the ladder, only to reach the third rung and have it crumble beneath her foot. The resulting fall knocked the breath out of her. When she looked up, Isaac was bending over her, she couldn't inhale, and her chest felt as if a two-ton grizzly was sitting on it.

"Suck up some air," he said.

His voice sounded as if it was coming from the bottom of that well out there. She turned her head to look in that direction and took several gasping breaths before her lungs stopped aching.

He gathered her up in his arms and carried her to the mound of hay where the cat had been hiding. "Are you hurt? Is anything broken?"

"Just my pride," she whispered.

He lowered his face to hers to hear her better. "What?"

"I said, only my pride."

His green eyes were closing in on her. She dropped her gaze to his mouth to keep from drowning in his eyes. When his lips brushed against hers, a shocking jolt sent her mind into a swirling eddy. So, that's what it was like to be kissed. No wonder Delia was so ready to marry Tyrell, if he'd sent her emotions into a whirlwind like that.

The second kiss was more than a peck and the shock even greater. When he broke if off, he turned away and said, "I'm sorry. That shouldn't have happened. I was scared you were dead."

She sat straight up. "I'm not one bit sorry. But you are right, it shouldn't have happened, and it won't again. I think I'll bed down right here. It's soft, and I can use my cape for a blanket. Good night, Isaac."

"Are you sure you're all right?"

She nodded. No, she wasn't all right. Her pride was hurt, and her mouth wanted more kisses to see if they all made beautiful music in her head and threw off a sweet glow inside her body. But her heart didn't want any more kisses from Isaac Burnet, because he was a man who might hurt her as Matthew had. Every thought was so confusing that she couldn't decide which one to listen to and which one to throw out into the well.

Fairlee hated not being able to control her emotions, and they'd been ripping around in confusing circles ever since the night she woke up in a ship with a storm going on all around her. She just wanted to go to sleep and forget everything.

CHAPTER EIGHT

They moved like shadows through a heavy fog, which was exactly like Fairlee's thoughts. One second she thought she had a firm reason for her feelings when Isaac had kissed her. The next, those reasons disappeared into the fog, and she couldn't reach out and get a hold on anything. She tried thinking about anything other than the kiss that had glued her firmly to the barn floor. The fall must have addled her temporarily, and that's what had bewildered her. It wasn't the effects of the kiss at all but the fact that she couldn't catch her breath after tumbling off the ladder.

Isaac had awakened her just after midnight for her watch. The minute she was fully awake, he'd claimed her spot in the hay and gone right to sleep. The kiss couldn't have sent him into a downward spiral as it had her, or he couldn't have been snoring in less than two minutes. All night while she was supposed to be sleeping, she'd worried about how they'd act toward each other. Would it be awkward? Would he apologize again? What would he say? How would he behave? For him to pretend nothing at all had happened was proving the worst of all.

She set her mouth in a firm line. She'd lost sleep and fretted all through her watch for nothing. That was enough to exhaust a saint's patience, and Fairlee Lavalle had never been accused of being a saint. Now they were riding, and it seemed as if they were getting nowhere, just like Fairlee's thoughts.

"You sure we're not going in circles? I think I saw that tree twice already this morning." She broke the uncomfortable silence.

He looked at his compass. "Lots of tall pine trees in this part of the country, so you might think you saw that one, but we've been moving north all morning."

She looked up, but the trees disappeared into the fog. "They're tall and straight. They'd make a good cabin."

Isaac followed her gaze all the way up and then back down. "My folks started out in a log cabin, and they kept it even after they built a real house. It's where my dad was when he was shot and killed. After Mother died, he went up there often. Said it reminded him of their first days together, when they struggled from daylight to dark just to get by."

Isaac had pondered how to go about talking about what had passed between them, but he didn't know how to approach the subject. He'd told her that it wouldn't happen again, and she'd been more than eager to agree. So the best thing was probably to let it alone. His father used to say that if you wanted the stink of a fresh cow pie to go away, you let the hot sun bake it; you didn't stir it with a stick.

"Does anyone live in the cabin now?" Fairlee asked.

"No. It's three miles from the house they eventually built and raised us two boys in. Way back at the edge of the plantation. We send someone up to give it a good cleaning a couple of times a year."

She wanted to talk more. About trees, fog, the cabin — anything to pass the time — but her mind went as blank as a sheet of writing paper. Finally she latched on to the night she was abducted and began a mental diary of all that had happened leading up to her kidnapping. Looking back with truth-improved vision on the events, she could now discern the gloom that had settled around the house like a funeral pall on the day before her wedding. Uncle Jonathan wasn't smiling and jolly the way he'd been when Delia married Tyrell. Aunt Rachel twisted her poor handkerchief into a ball so many times that the tatted lace raveled on the edges. Tempie fussed and fumed and told Fairlee that she was making a big mistake.

Finally that day had ended. The parlor was decorated and ready for the wedding. The preacher and his wife were sleeping in the east wing. Matthew and his family would arrive the next morning, and Fanny had the cake made and ready to frost. Nothing could possibly go wrong.

"But it did," she mumbled.

"What did you say?" Isaac asked quickly. Time stood still, and he wanted to talk or listen — either, just to make it move again.

"Nothing," she said.

He sighed.

She went back to that evening. Tempie's spirits had risen when they were in Fairlee's bedroom. Now Fairlee knew why. Tempie's job had been to see to it that Fairlee drank all the drugged tea so that Isaac could more easily abduct her. After that things got as foggy as the soup they were traveling through that morning. Until she awoke on the ship — to the storm and to Isaac Burnet.

She went back over all that had happened since, a day at a time. They'd reached their first stop on Thursday. *No, it was Friday,* she argued with herself. She'd slept a whole night and day and awoke from the drugged sleep the next night.

Her brow drew down into a furrow as she went back over each day again. She distinctly remembered the date on the hotel register, and it said Thursday. She retraced the days a third time.

"You sorry scoundrel! You lied to me!" she said.

"I did not. We are headed due north," Isaac protested.

"You said I'd been asleep for a whole day and night, but it was only a few hours. I had time to get back to my wedding if I'd ridden hard, and no one would have been the wiser," she blurted out.

He chuckled. "Took you a while to figure that one out, didn't it? I was just buying you some time to come to your senses."

She clamped her mouth shut and refused to speak to him again. They ate cold biscuits stuffed with leftover bacon and potatoes for their noon meal, and she didn't say a word. He shot a wild turkey that appeared right in their path in the middle of the afternoon, and they roasted it for supper. Still she didn't speak to him.

"So, how long are you going to do this silent treatment?" he asked.

"Until I'm not mad anymore," she said.

"Got any idea how long that'll be?"

"Until three days past eternity."

"Suits me just fine. I don't like a chattering woman anyway. Go on and get some sleep. I'll pick the turkey meat off the bones for tomorrow," he said.

"I can do that on my watch. It'll give me something to do," she argued.

"For a woman who wasn't going to talk, you sure are ready to fight with me."

"Pick the turkey, then. I'm going to sleep."

She curled up against a fallen tree, using her cape for a cover and her saddle for a pillow. It wasn't as comfortable as the soft pile of hay in the barn, but as least it wasn't raining. The moon hung in the sky, the stars twinkling all around it. The fog was gone, and everything was as clear as crystal. At least weather-wise. Fairlee didn't know if her life would be that clear ever again.

Day three.

A tickle in Isaac's throat gave him a slight cough all day. At noon he pulled out the bottle of whiskey he'd bought more to rile Fairlee than anything else and took a long swig, hoping to cauterize the raw feeling.

"Well, at least you lasted three days without needing the liquor," she said.

"Add the week before to that for a more accurate number," he said.

That evening his cough was worse, and he took another sip after they'd eaten skillet cornbread and the last of the turkey.

"Drinking again?" she asked.

"Sore throat," he admitted.

The hair on the back of her neck stood straight up. What would she do if he got sick or, heaven forbid, died? She was in strange country and knew no one. Granted, she'd made her brag that she could take care of herself, but the thought of being alone under such circumstances, or responsible for an ailing giant who wouldn't be easy to maneuver, was terrifying.

"Go get some rest. I'll take first watch. I made enough cornbread for breakfast," she said.

"It's going to hurt whether I'm asleep or awake. If we upset our routine, we'll both be exhausted," he said.

She didn't argue but opted to sleep behind the tree where he'd sat down with his gun across his lap. She slept lightly and heard every cough.

Day four.

Isaac drank three cups of coffee for breakfast but ate very little. Fairlee kept a close watch on him all morning. He slept the whole time when they stopped for their noon meal. That evening his cough was worse, even though he said his throat felt better. She forced him to drink another slug of whiskey and insisted on taking first watch.

"I don't care if it messes up our routine. If you don't get some serious rest, you could get sick enough to die," she said.

"Not before I get you home to Delia. A Burnet does not go back on his word," he croaked.

When he went to sleep, she covered him with her cape and snuggled down into her coat. It was well after midnight when the horses became restless and woke her from a doze. She sat straight up and carefully scanned the area.

"Hello the camp!" someone yelled from out in the darkness.

Isaac didn't stir.

"Who are you?" she yelled back.

"Five hungry men. Do you have food to share?"

"We do not. We do have sickness. Either

pox or fever. Take your pick if you want to come any closer," she said.

"I don't believe her. It's two women traveling together, and they're trying to scare us off," a deeper voice said.

"Believe me or not. My husband is ill, and we're just trying to get home before he dies. Come on in if you've got a mind to rob us, but remember you'll be taking away something that you don't want," she said.

Isaac started coughing and couldn't stop. It sounded as if he was dying of consumption, and Fairlee feared that he really might die before he could stop.

"Let's get out of here. Horses and that mule ain't worth dyin' for," the deep-voiced man said.

"I say they're fakin'," the other said.

"I don't care what either of you do. I'm making a big circle around them people. I saw my brother die in Texas of that stuff. They cough up blood and can't breathe and die a horrible death like they're drowning. I ain't takin' chances," a third voice said.

She heard horses' hooves but no more conversation. Then the night was eerily still again.

"They gone?" Isaac whispered.

"I think so."

He threw back the cape and stretched.

"Was I convincing?"

"It worked, but it was mean. I thought you were dying," she said breathlessly.

He laughed down deep in his chest. "Did you care?"

"I'm not even going to answer that."

The laughter stopped, and he coughed several times before he got it under control. "Get some sleep," he said.

"I'd rather mount up and ride in the opposite direction of those men. They could come back and shoot us from a distance and take our horses and mules anyway. Besides, I'm too nervous to sleep."

"You're probably right. We'll stop early tomorrow and get some really good sleep."

In thirty minutes they were back in the saddle and riding due north again. She kept looking behind her, and every time Isaac coughed, she checked his lips for signs of blood.

Day five.

"I've got my bearings now. I know where we are. There'll be a deserted house up ahead. Settlers moved in and couldn't make a go of it, so they sold out and moved on. The plantation owner who bought it uses it for an outpost cabin in the winter. If he's not there, he won't mind if we hole up in it until tomorrow," Isaac said.

"How much farther to Delia's?" Fairlee asked. One minute she was freezing, the next minute she was sweating. She was coming down with something, but it didn't bring on a sore throat, so the kiss hadn't caused it.

"Two hard days' ride," he said.

Two more days, and then she could sleep for a week if she wanted to. Delia would have good food and warm beds. Then everything would be fine. Isaac would go on to his home, and she wouldn't have to think of the kiss every time she looked at him.

The settler's house was only a one-room cabin, but it had a good fireplace with dry wood racked up beside it. A straw-filled mattress covered with a quilt was shoved up against the wall opposite the fireplace. Two mismatched chairs and a small table occupied a corner under a boarded-over broken window.

Isaac set about building a fire, and Fairlee brought in their supplies. When he had a blaze going, he took the horses out to the barn, fed and watered them, and came back to the house.

Warmth and the aroma of frying bacon hit Isaac when he opened the cabin door. He was tired enough to sleep without food, and Fairlee was as pale as the second day's fog they'd traveled through. If she didn't sleep, she was going to be sick when he delivered her to Delia.

I didn't promise that she'd be in excellent health, just that I wouldn't let her marry Cheval, he thought.

A sharp prick to his conscience brought him up short. He'd pushed her too hard, especially after the drugged sleep. The boat had been damp, and the next week in drafty old stagecoaches hadn't been much better. Now they'd been five days out in the open. It was a wonder she hadn't gotten sick before then.

"We don't need to set up a watch tonight. The horses and mule are safe in the barn. We can both sleep," he said.

She'd peeled the last two potatoes, and they had browned up nicely in the bacon drippings. She scooped them out onto a plate with the rest of the bacon and poured bread dough into the skillet. When it had browned on the bottom, she flipped it over and put a lid on the top.

"Did you hear me?" Isaac asked.

She nodded. "If you'll watch that for ten minutes, it will be done. I don't want to eat. I just want to sleep."

She sat down on the edge of the mattress

and removed her boots, pulled the cape over her, and shut her eyes. "Wake me when it's time to make breakfast."

"Are you sick?" he asked.

"Just very tired," she answered.

He pulled a bottle from the supply sack and handed it to her. "I want you to take a slug of the whiskey. It'll warm you from the inside and ward off sickness."

The fact that she didn't argue with him convinced him that she *was* sick. She propped herself up on an elbow and reached for the bottle. She tilted it back, swallowed a mouthful, and shivered to her bare toes. "That is sin in a bottle. Why do men drink that vile stuff?"

He wiped off the neck of the bottle and took a slug. "My throat is better, and my cough nearly gone. It might be wicked, but it kills off sickness."

"Nothing can survive fire — that's what it is." She lay back and shut her eyes again, only to dream fretfully of Isaac dying and leaving her to find her own way to Delia's.

Day six.

Fairlee awoke to the noise of a crackling fire and something frying. She threw off the cape, but her toes were freezing. She hurriedly put on stockings and boots and stood up, only to have the floor move toward her face and the rest of the room spin around like a top. She grabbed for a chair and sat down.

"Still feeling poorly?" Isaac turned in time to see her sink into a chair, her eyes rolling around as if she were trying to focus on anything at all.

"Is this what it feels like to be drunk?" she asked.

He laughed. "Darlin', one little sip of whiskey won't make you drunk. And even if you drank the whole bottle, it would be worn off by now. All you'd have is a headache."

"Don't call me darlin'."

"Yes, ma'am! I went out to take care of the animals and shot two rabbits. That's our breakfast. There was plenty of bread left from last night," he said.

"I'm not hungry."

He piled the meat onto a plate and set it between them. "Doesn't matter. If you don't eat, you'll be even dizzier. It's a long time between now and dinner. If we can catch the ferry tomorrow evening before it shuts down for the night, we can be home. So eat, Fairlee."

She picked up a rabbit haunch and bit into it. The meat was hot and tender, but she had no appetite. Each bite was a chore to chew and a bigger one to swallow. The last time she had felt so poorly, Aunt Rachel had put her to bed for a week and called the doctor. He'd prescribed a vile-tasting liquid and wouldn't let Tempie or Delia into the room with her.

Just two more days and this horrid journey would be finished.

"Do you think the time will ever come when people can travel faster than stagecoaches and horseback?" she asked.

"Yes, I do. In a hundred years it'll be amazing what will have changed. But today we have to depend on our horses and pack mule. Supplies are getting low, so it's a good thing we're nearly there. Got enough flour for one more pan of bread, but the bacon and grease are both gone. We'll need to do some hunting today on the way," Isaac told her.

"Is there a house like this at the end of the day?" she asked.

"Not a house, but the ferryman has a barn he'll let us use if we make it there before he stops for the night," Isaac answered.

Fairlee kept her back straight all day, but the last hour it was a chore. She ached from her toenails to her scalp. There were places on her body she didn't even realize could hurt, but they did.

They reached the ferry just as it was getting ready to make its last run for the day. Isaac bought a slab of ham from the man's wife and a gallon of milk for their supper.

Fairlee ate a few bites and drank half a cup of milk before she went to sleep again. She refused to take a sip of the whiskey, saying that it hadn't done anything but make her stomach burn the night before.

Isaac ate and stretched out in the hay only a foot from her. Her breathing was normal, but her color was even grayer than it had been the night before. She was definitely sick, and he had to decide whether to take her on to Delia's or to his house, which was closer. Either way someone would be exposed to the illness. Either Delia and her unborn child or Micah.

"I don't want to go," she mumbled in her sleep.

"Where?" he asked gently.

"Don't try to talk me into it. I don't want to go to Texas, Tempie."

"Why?"

"I'm afraid," she mumbled.

He threw an arm over her and moved closer. "Don't be afraid. I'll take care of you," he whispered.

"Don't leave me."

"Never," he said.

She sighed and slept soundly.

Isaac spent the next two hours trying to make sense of his feelings.

Day seven.

Fairlee wouldn't eat breakfast or lunch, and by the time they were on Burnet property, she was sagging in the saddle with her chin against her chest as she slipped in and out of fitful sleep.

Isaac knew he couldn't take her to Delia's, but he couldn't take her to his house either. There was only one alternative, and it was actually closer than either of the other two places. Dark clouds gave way to a fine, cold mist, but he pushed on. Three more miles and he'd have her at the cabin.

"I can't do it, Isaac. We've got to stop," she said.

"Another hour," he said.

"I can't."

He reined up and slid off his horse and gathered her into his arms when she tumbled from her mount. His horse was tired but strong enough to carry them both for a few miles. It took three tries to get back into the saddle without dropping her, but he made it and kept going.

She was burning up with fever and glistened with sweat from it. The heat from her body made him feel as if he was carrying a bucket of hot coals next to his chest.

When he saw the log cabin in the distance, he wanted to shout but was afraid he'd startle her. Rain had started in earnest by the time he carried her inside and into the one bedroom. He laid her on the bed, tucked the cape in around her, and headed for the woodpile outside the back door. Fire first to chase away the chill. Taking care of the animals second. They could wait. He wasn't sure that Fairlee could.

She was on a bed, a real one. That meant that they'd made it to Delia's. Now everything would be fine. She'd sleep until morning, and then she and Delia would laugh and talk about her adventure. She couldn't wait to tell her all about the potential robbers she and Isaac had put to route with the story of a contagious fever.

No, no! She couldn't be at Delia's. What if she gave her the fever, and the baby died? She sat straight up in bed. Everything was spinning around her, but she had to get out of the house.

The fire looked inviting when she went to the living room. Somehow she'd thought Delia lived in a much bigger house than this little cottage. She'd imagined it to look more like their plantation, if on a slightly smaller scale. This was just a glorified cabin.

"Delia?" she called out.

No one answered, and she breathed a sigh of relief. Delia must be off visiting or at least outside in the fresh air, taking care of her garden. Summer was such a busy time of year for a plantation owner's wife. Fairlee frowned as she made her way toward the front door. When had winter and spring gone and summer arrived?

She remembered it was winter when she and Isaac were traveling to Mississippi, but now it was summer. It had to be, because she was sweating, and it was so very hot in the house. A blast of cold wind hit her in the face when she opened the door. Now, that was strange. She took a step outside, and cool rain swept over her. It felt wonderful against her burning skin.

Isaac screamed her name as he flew up the steps. His feet were scarcely touching the ground, and his voice had been loud but was fading away, as if it were coming from the bottom of that stone well at the back of the house. She took two more steps, and suddenly strong arms lifted her up into the air. And that was the last thing she remembered for two days.

CHAPTER NINE

Fairlee awoke and took in her surroundings. The room was half the size of her bedroom in Louisiana, but it didn't have the impersonal feel of a hotel room. People had lived in this room, not just visited it. She could feel love surrounding her. A washstand with a pretty pitcher and bowl on it was in the far corner. A rocking chair drawn up beside the bed held cloth strips and the beginning of a rag rug. She turned her head to find a rocking chair on the other side with a book on the seat.

Her hair was neatly twined into two long braids that fell down across her body, which wore a snowy white nightgown. She felt as if she was floating on clouds in the feather bed, but where was she, and how had she gotten there? Had she died? Was this heaven?

A beautiful soprano voice filtered in from the other room. Fairlee recognized the song.

Their cook sang it often while she worked, but her voice wasn't as high or as clear as this one. The song was called "Roll, Jordon, Roll," and the singer sang about the trumpets blowing her home to the new Jerusalem. When the singer finished that one, she went right into "Jehovah, Hallelujah," about the foxes needing no holes and the birdies needing no nests. Fairlee pinched her arm to make sure she was still among the living. It hurt like the dickens, so she figured she hadn't started up to the pearly gates just yet.

The aroma of food wafted in through the open door, and Fairlee licked her dry lips. She was so very thirsty. She looked around again and spied a water pitcher and glass on a small table beside the bed. She tried to reach for it but knocked the glass to the floor, making a terrible noise.

The doorway darkened immediately, and her eyes widened in fear. Would she be punished for making a mess in heaven? But, no, she was among the living, wasn't she? She frowned as she tried to remember when it was that she'd pinched herself. Was it before or after she'd died?

"Are you awake, Miz Fairlee?" the woman asked. Her voice sounded clear and sweet, like that of a young woman, but she was as old as a huge oak tree and about as sturdy looking. Her curly hair, pulled back into a bun at the nape of her neck, was almost totally white, a contrast to the round ebony face with big brown eyes and wide cheeks.

"Where am I?" Fairlee whispered.

"Oh, my Lord, the fever has done something to your mind," the woman said.

"My brain is fine. I just don't know where I am. Is this Delia's house?"

The woman raised her huge arms. "Praise the Lord! This ain't Delia's house. This is the old cabin. I'm Mama Glory, and Miz Delia sent me to see you through the fever." She picked up the glass, which hadn't broken, and filled it with water.

"Thank goodness the glass didn't break!"

"I reckon Mr. Isaac wouldn't care if you broke a dozen of them fancy glasses. He's been worried nigh to death about you." She picked Fairlee up as if she was nothing but a little girl's rag doll and held the water to her lips.

Fairlee gulped twice before Mama Glory took it away.

"You shouldn't have too much. Take two sips ever' ten minutes, or you'll be throwin' it all up, and it won't do you a bit of good." The woman wasn't much taller than Fairlee, but she was as wide as she was tall, and her tone didn't allow for argument.

Fairlee licked her lips to get the last few drops. "How long have I been here?"

"Two days. Mr. Isaac rode 'til he found Mr. Micah in the fields and sent him to bring me. I know about the fever. Now that it's gone, you'll be weak as a kitten for two more days, then you can get up and move a little each day until you're strong enough to go to Miz Delia's."

"How long will that take?"

"It'll be a month before I let you go to the big house," Mama Glory said.

"A month!" Fairlee gasped.

Mama Glory eased herself down in the rocking chair. "I'll be stayin' for two more days, and then I'll go on back. Miz Delia might need me if that baby comes early. I got to be there to bring it into the world."

"A month," Fairlee groaned.

"I ain't takin' no chances. I won't have Miz Delia gettin' what you had, and you don't want your sister to get it either. It'd kill the baby for sure. Mr. Tyrell would lose his mind if anything happened to her or that baby," Mama Glory said.

"Mama Glory? Is dinner about ready?" Isaac called from the doorway.

"Wipe your feet. I just mopped that floor. Miz Fairlee woke up!" She talked as she heaved herself up from the rocking chair and lumbered across the floor.

A smile tickled the corners of Fairlee's mouth. Mama Glory sounded just like Fanny. Oftentimes Fairlee wondered who the real bosses were on the plantations. Fanny ran the household and the kitchen like a dictator. Evidently Mama Glory did the same here.

Isaac leaned on the doorjamb and stared at Fairlee propped up in bed. She was still as pale as the sheets covering her, but her eyes weren't glazed with fever any longer. Mama Glory said it would take two full days to see if she'd live or pass on, that it was up to Fairlee to make up her mind which one she wanted to do.

"Guess you decided to live," he said.

He sure didn't sound as if he'd been worried out of his mind to Fairlee. Standing there, all masculine with that little smirk on his face, he seemed to be saying that he'd gotten her onto the Fannin and Burnet land, so his job was finished.

"Guess I did," she said. "What happened there at the end? I don't remember much except feeling horrible."

"You started coming down with the fever a couple of days before we made it here. Barely got you inside before you passed out.

I hated to leave you, but we needed help, so I put you on the bed and took off for the house. Met Micah in the field, and he sent me back. He brought Mama Glory in a wagon in a couple of hours. She chased me out of the bedroom and took care of you," he said.

"Won't Mama Glory catch the fever?"

Isaac frowned. "Aren't you worried about me?"

"If you were going to come down with it, you already would have. You kissed me," she said.

Mama Glory pretended she didn't hear that comment, but a smile erased most of the wrinkles around her eyes. She started singing her spirituals again as she dipped up Isaac's dinner. Yes, sir, in two days she was going home. They didn't need her meddling in things that had already gotten started.

"Shh." He rolled his eyes toward the kitchen.

"You didn't answer me about Mama Glory," Fairlee said. She was getting tired of sitting up, and her eyes were drooping.

"Mama Glory has nursed every fever patient on this farm back to health. Mother brought her to this part when she and Daddy married. Mama Glory had been her nurse when she was a baby, and she brought all three of us boys into the world. Tyrell and Delia begged her to stay with them when they got married, but she wouldn't leave me and Micah until Delia announced there was going to be a baby. Then she packed up her things and moved — after she gave her daughter strict instructions on how to keep things going at our house. So, no, she's not going to catch it. She's too mean and cantankerous to get the fever," Isaac said.

"I might be old and mean, but I still got mighty good hearin'. You want your dinner burned or not?"

Isaac winked at Fairlee. "Sorry, Mama Glory. Me and Micah just miss you, and I'm grumbling."

"Well, you get on in here and get set up to the table. I'm goin' to feed Miz Fairlee. By suppertime I expect she'll be able to do for herself, but right now she's weak," she said.

She brought a cup of rich potato soup into the room and set it on the washstand while she draped a tea towel across Fairlee's chest. "You'll go slow. Your innards won't take much today, and if you eat too fast, it'll come back up just as fast."

Fairlee had eaten potato soup all her life,

but that first bite was pure heaven. She chewed the small chunks of potatoes slowly and enjoyed the buttery flavor of the milk-based soup. It was a good thing that Mama Glory was feeding her, or she'd have wolfed down the whole cupful in less than two minutes.

"Enough for now. In the middle of the afternoon you can have more," Mama Glory said after a few more sips.

"Just one more," Fairlee pleaded.

Mama Glory smiled. "Isaac, please tell this woman of yours what it means when I say no."

"She ain't my woman, but it means no. Mama Glory don't ever change her mind. No is no. Yes is yes."

"I am *not* his woman," Fairlee said through gritted teeth.

Mama Glory headed back to the kitchen. "I heard both of you."

Isaac finished his dinner and went back to the bedroom. "I'm going back out to help Micah. Mama Glory will take care of whatever you need this afternoon."

"Mmm," Fairlee muttered without opening her eyes. She could take care of herself. She didn't need either of them now that the fever had gone.

She awoke ravenous and thirsty. All three

of Mama Glory's chins rested on her chest, and her rag rug had fallen from her hands to the floor. Fairlee threw back the quilt and eased her feet off the bed. When she stood up, everything started twirling, and a buzz like that of a giant bumblebee filled her ears.

Mama Glory grabbed her as she wilted and laid her back on the bed. "You don't get to do that until tomorrow. Then it's with help, and only to the rockin' chair up in front of the fire. You got to pay attention to my orders, or you still won't make it," she scolded.

"I'm hungry and thirsty," Fairlee said.

"And it's time for the medicine. Got to get food down first, then the medicine. Got to take it two more days. It don't taste good, but it'll make you well." Mama Glory hurried off to the kitchen.

She brought back a thick slice of bread slathered with butter and honey and a cup of hot tea. "You eat two bites and then take the medicine. After that you can have some sweet honey tea to get the taste out of your mouth."

Fairlee eyed the square bottle and the spoon. "What is it?"

"It's my magic." Mama Glory laughed.

"Does it taste very bad?"

"You been takin' it with a little broth for

197

the past two days. It didn't kill you then, and it won't now. Yes, it's bitter, and it'll make you wish you was still asleep, but you got today and tomorrow before your doses are all done."

Fairlee waved her away. "I don't want it. I'm better. I don't need it."

Mama Glory laughed again. "Who's the biggest, me or you? You will take this medicine. One spoonful today and one tomorrow. After I see you take the one tomorrow, I'm going home, and you won't have to take no more. You won't get this fever but one time in your life. Once you get it, then it's over, so you don't have to worry about ever havin' it again."

"Why didn't Isaac get it? He was coughing. Make him take the stuff too," Fairlee said.

Mama Glory pulled off a small piece of bread and put it into Fairlee's mouth. "The honey will coat your mouth and make it go down a little easier. I don't waste my medicine. Isaac doesn't have what you have. He had it when he was a little boy, so he won't get it again. This ain't for a cough. I got a different one for that. This is for the Indian Fever." Mama Glory carefully filled the spoon.

Fairlee took a deep breath and opened her

mouth to accept the potion. After she'd painfully swallowed the stuff, she must have been a sight, with her flared nostrils, her wide blue eyes, and her mouth all puckered up as if she'd just sucked on a raw green persimmon, because Mama Glory laughed until she had to wipe her eyes with her big calico apron.

"That'll sure enough make the old fever go away and die," she sputtered between hiccups.

When Fairlee could catch her breath and stop shuddering, she said, "You're right. No fever could survive that awful stuff. What's in it?"

"My mama showed me how to make it when I was a little girl. Way back before they stole me away and brought me across the big water on the ship. I was in my thirteenth year. When I was in my sixteenth year they needed me to help Mister Isaac's momma. I been with this family all that time, and ain't nobody ever talked me into tellin' what was in my medicine. When I'm dyin', I'll tell my daughter. That's the way of it. Now you're going to finish up this bread and tea, and come suppertime you'll be ready for something a little stronger."

Fairlee didn't argue when Mama Glory raised more bread toward her mouth, but when she held the cup up to her lips, Fairlee clutched it with both hands. "I can do this much," she said.

"That's a good sign. Tomorrow you're goin' to get dressed. Layin' in bed too long will make you weak." Mama Glory continued to feed her bites of bread.

Fairlee drew her brow into a frown. "Where did I get this nightgown? I didn't pack one when we left the hotel. Oh, no . . . Did . . . ?"

Mama Glory patted her arm. "I washed you myself and put that gown on you. Woman shouldn't be wearin' britches like you was. Besides, they was dirty. I tore 'em up for this rug I been workin' on, once they was washed clean of the grime and dirt."

Fairlee continued to frown. "But where did it come from? Did you bring it from Delia's?"

"Nope, got it out of that trunk over there. Belonged to Mister Isaac's momma. She and his papa came up here sometimes, and she kept things here. She was about your size. Kind of like you. Hair not as dark, and green-eyed instead of blue. But spirited like you," Mama Glory said.

"You really cut my trousers up for a rag rug?" Fairlee asked.

Mama Glory pointed a finger at her.

"Menfolk wear britches. Ladies wear dresses. Might be the hand of God that struck you with the Indian Fever for wearin' them kind of things."

"I don't believe that," Fairlee said.

"Don't matter what you believe. What matters is the truth. Drink your tea. It's got honey in it, and it'll help heal you up."

Fairlee sipped the last of the tea and handed the cup to Mama Glory. "Do I really have to stay here a whole month? I'll be fine in a week, and I'm not contagious when there's no fever. I want to see Delia. Please."

"Ain't no amount of beggin' going to make me say yes. I say a month, I mean a month. You can get your strength back by cooking and cleanin' for Mister Isaac."

Fairlee slapped the covers. "Isaac can go home with you. I'll take care of myself. I don't need him around."

Mama Glory set her jaw and narrowed her eyes. "He will be stayin' right here. He ain't bringin' no Indian Fever to my new baby. And you can just put up with him. A month ain't so long anyway."

Fairlee exhaled loudly.

"I don't care if you are a woman with a mind of her own and you don't carry on like a spoiled little girl. You blow out at me again that way, and I'll make you take another dose of medicine," Mama Glory said.

"Yes, ma'am. I'm sorry." Fairlee felt like a little girl who'd upset Fanny again. "But I still don't see why *he* has to stay. You know what people will say. Please let him go on back, and you stay with me. You could carry the disease as much as he can."

Mama Glory shook her head slowly. "I know how to clean it off me. Mister Isaac stays, and I go. Now, that's all there's goin' to be about that."

CHAPTER TEN

Fairlee watched from the window as Micah drove Mama Glory away in a wagon. He'd brought supplies but left them on the porch, just like Mama Glory had told him to do. A cured ham, a slab of bacon, milk, eggs, and several loaves of fresh bread from his kitchen. Isaac took the meat and milk to the well house where it would stay cold and brought the bread and eggs into the cabin.

She picked up the rug Mama Glory had been working on and braided several strips of cloth together. When it was finished, it would be an oval of dark, serviceable colors, not a fancy rug to go in front of the fireplace but one that would catch dirt at the front door. She winced when she recognized the fabric from her trousers.

Isaac stomped dirt from his boots at the door and carried in a load of wood. He put a log in the fireplace and threw in a handful of kindling. It sparked, and soon the log was blazing.

"Looks like it could snow or pour down rain any minute," he said.

"Why didn't you tell Mama Glory to send another woman out here to stay with me? You don't have to be here. You can go home. You were out there twice with Micah, so Mama Glory doesn't think you are a carrier of the fever. Why are you here?"

"Got to see it through, Fairlee. I told Delia I'd deliver you to her parlor. A Burnet's word is good as gold. We stand by it," he said. He didn't say that the kiss they'd shared had jarred his heart and soul, that he wanted to spend time with her to find out what it meant, and that he'd really had no choice, because Mama Glory had declared it, and no one argued with her.

"I'm ruined," she said.

"Guess you are."

"It's not fair that we can stay in this cabin together and you can still take a wife and be happy, but I'll always have a shadow following me," she told him.

"Life isn't fair. If it was, I wouldn't have ever met you sisters in the first place," he said. That he meant with his whole heart. It would have been so much easier if a bandit hadn't killed his father, if he and Micah and

Tyrell hadn't set off to catch him and bring him to justice, if they hadn't gotten into the fight in a San Antonio cantina and wound up in jail.

"What are we going to do for a whole month?" she groaned.

"I guess we'll live one day at a time and figure it out as we go," he answered.

"Why does Mama Glory get to decide how long until I can go to Delia's?"

He sat down in the rocker beside Fairlee and set it into a slow, easy motion. "She's taken care of more fever victims than you can count. She brews her own medicine with herbs she gathers in the springtime. It's something she learned when she was a girl. There's lots of kinds of fevers. She seems to know which is which. Call it magic if you want, but if she'd said my father was to stay in his room for a month, he wouldn't have questioned her word. Mother said she was an angel and we were all lucky to have her."

"She always that bossy?" Fairlee asked.

Isaac nodded. "She was like a grandmother to us. She used to tell us that we had to mind our mother and father, that their word was to be obeyed. But her word, of course, was the law."

"Like Fanny," Fairlee said.

"Makes you wonder who's really the boss, don't it?" He smiled.

Her heart did a double backflip and skipped a beat. Nothing made a bit of sense. The man she had been about to marry had never affected her the way Isaac did when his eyes lit up in a smile.

"Well, she's gone, and we might as well get on with the day," she tried to say calmly. "She said you were to cook today and that tomorrow I can manage the kitchen but not to be doing anything that would tax my strength. At least she let me get dressed." Fairlee looked down at the dark blue dress that Mama Glory had removed from the trunk. It was a wee bit long but otherwise fit her fine.

"It was Mother's dress. I remember it well. It matches your eyes nicely," he said.

Her silly heart did another of those flips. Not once had Matthew ever noticed if she was wearing something that matched her eyes. They'd talked about renovating his drafty old house and the gardens she planned to put in when spring came. He'd been attentive in those things and had once said that he would be glad when they were married. He'd even had a wistful look in his eyes, but he hadn't been looking at her.

She kept her eyes on the long, braided

ropes she was stitching into an oval. "Thank you."

"Want me to read to you while you sew? I remember that my father used to do that while Mother sewed beside the fireplace in the winter," he said.

"What are you reading?" She liked the sound of his voice, and it would be nice to listen to a story to pass the time.

"It's a book of short stories called *Evenings on a Farm near Dikanka.* I've read it dozens of times, but I always find something funny in the tales when I reread them. I'll read the first one about a fair at Sorochintsy."

"Where the devil is that?"

He smiled again. "Strange that you should put it that way, because there is a devil involved. I'll read it, and then you can tell me what you think."

She tried to listen to the story about a peasant who went to the fair to sell wheat with his wife and daughter, but her mind kept drifting back to the kiss. Isaac read about a haunted barn, a devil on a quest for a lost jacket, and other evil happenings out there in the world on his way to Sorochintsy.

"The end," he said when he finished.

"Do you really believe there's such things as haunted barns and houses?" she asked.

He shut the book and laid it aside. "You're questioning *my* story, when you and your sisters were Indian witches? Even tried to stake poor little Tempest in the flames to see if she could survive it."

"We weren't really going to light her up. We were just playing," Fairlee said.

"We'll never really know, since your mother rescued her. But to answer your question, I don't believe in haunted houses like in the story. But I believe that memories live on in houses and places. I'm sure that's why my father kept coming back to this cabin. He remembered those first exciting moments with my mother here, and in the memories he could imagine her still here, maybe sitting in front of the fire in that dress and making a rag rug. He could sit where I am, and she'd be there. He could even talk to her, and, knowing her the way he did, he would know what she'd answer, so in his mind they could have had conversations."

Fairlee looked down at the rug and the dress. Did she remind Isaac of his mother? Good Lord! She didn't want him to think of his mother when he looked at her.

"Then you don't believe in ghosts?"

He laughed. "No, not in creepy, scary shadows that walk in the night and scare little children."

"Then what?" she asked.

"Memories again. My father was killed not far from this house. If I go out there, I can still see him lyin' in the dirt, facedown, a bullet hole in his back. He's not there anymore, of course. We buried him. But I can still see him, so still and not breathing, and my heart hurts just like it did that day. Not a ghost, exactly, but a very real memory. Do you believe in ghosts?"

Fairlee hesitated a long time before she spoke. "Not really, but I've had doubts. Sometimes I can hear my mother's voice speaking to me, and I can actually feel my father in the room with me. I like what you said about it being a memory surfacing. That makes sense to me."

He stood up and stretched, bending to each side. "Body gets stiff if it sits too long."

Fairlee laid her sewing aside. "Mama Glory said she left soup on the stove. I'll help you get it onto the table for dinner."

Isaac shook his head emphatically. "No, ma'am. Today you are to sit in the chair by the fire, walk to the table, sit some more, and then go to bed. Tomorrow you get to spread your wings and fly a little bit."

"Angels fly. Remember, I'm no angel. If I recall correctly, you said that wine got

209

turned to water when we Lavalle girls changed from our habits to our trousers." She headed toward the kitchen.

He put a hand on her shoulder when she reached the table and pulled out a chair. "That's as far as you go. I gave Mama Glory my word."

"You can take your word and go to . . ." Fairlee's blue eyes flashed with pure old Lavalle mad.

He put a finger over her lips. "Don't say it."

His touch burned her lips more than the fever had tormented her body. One part of her wanted to bite his hand; the other part wanted to kiss his finger.

"Just sit down, and let me take care of the meal today. It's only heating a pot of beef stew and serving it with cornbread," he said.

"This is the last day I'm an invalid," she declared.

He set the pot of soup onto the burner and stoked up the embers in the firebox set at chest level. "Yes, it is, and before the month is over, you'll be whining that you want to go back to being waited on. When you do, I'll remind you of this day."

"*If* I do, you can remind me, and I won't even kick you in the shins for it. I'm surprised to see a cookstove in a cabin. I would have thought they'd have cooked over the fireplace," she said.

He added a chunk of wood. "They did in the beginning, when they lived here. But as soon as Mother heard about these cookstoves, she had one shipped for the house they'd built by then. Then when a new and better model came out, she got that and put this one in here. Mama Glory likes this one better because it's the one she learned to use. Took a while to get her to give up her hooks and pots for the fireplace, but once she made up her mind, she loved it."

"Same story with Fanny. Aunt Rachel had to talk long and hard to make her go anywhere near the new stove when it came. I was still a little girl. Fanny declared that the cookstove was the work of the devil, that nothing that big and black could have come from anywhere but hell." Fairlee giggled.

It was like tinkling cymbals to Isaac's ears. He wished he had something clever to say to make her keep laughing, but he couldn't think of a thing, and that aggravated him. He stirred the soup until it bubbled, carried the cast-iron pot to the table, and set it on a wooden trivet that his father had carved out of a stump back when he first built the cabin.

"I'll get the bowls and bread," she said.

He put a hand on her shoulder. "Tomorrow."

She folded her arms over her chest. "I hate that word."

His eyes sparkled, and his mouth turned up in a grin. It was the first time she'd noticed that his lips told different stories. The thinner top one belonged on a man with a firm, serious demeanor. The fuller bottom lip belonged on a happy-go-lucky sort of fellow.

"Get used to it," he said. "There's about four weeks of them in store before we can get on with our lives."

She sat still and thought about his lips. His chin went with his upper lip, his eyes with the lower one. His high cheekbones and forehead went with his upper lip, his jawline with the lower one. Maybe Isaac Burnet was like an onion — she'd have to peel the layers to find out what was in the center.

Well, she had a whole month to peel, and, with luck, when she reached the inner core, she'd find that she didn't like Isaac at all.

CHAPTER ELEVEN

Wind whistled through the tree branches, knocking a few big pecan limbs down onto the roof of the cabin to rattle around like someone doing a barn dance in work boots. Fairlee washed the breakfast dishes and wished Delia would at least send a cook and maid to her aid. Surely there were a few servants who had already suffered through the Indian Fever and wouldn't catch it again.

She sighed as she put away the last plate and put a chicken into a pot to boil. She'd make dumplings for dinner along with baked sweet potatoes. She might fry some doughnuts if she got bored with sewing the rug Mama Glory had started and left behind. She'd washed on Monday, ironed on Tuesday, and here it was Wednesday of the second week, and the cabin walls were closing in on her.

It was a fair-sized place with a big living

room and kitchen combined. Crisp calico curtains graced the windows looking out onto the porch that wrapped around two sides. The kitchen door opened out onto a stoop, with a woodpile stacked against the house on the left and several lilac bushes on the right. In the spring they'd give off a wonderful aroma that would waft into the house every time someone fanned in or out the door. A stone fireplace covered the north wall of the living room, and Isaac always left it blazing before he went out after breakfast.

The bedroom where she slept ran the length of the house on the west side but was only half as wide as the living quarters. She crossed the kitchen and living room and stood in the doorway of her room. The bed was made, her nightgown folded and put away — nothing to do in that room.

She went to her rocking chair and picked up the rags, braided a few, and then threw them down. Up again, to the kitchen to check the chicken, which was cooking nicely, to the wood in the stove, which was fine, to the window to see what was going on outside, and back to the bedroom. If she didn't get out of the house soon, Mama Glory was going to have to figure out a dose of something to cure cabin fever.

She eyed the ladder set at a forty-five degree angle up to the loft where Isaac disappeared every night. She never saw him descend because he was already up and gone to take care of the animals before she made it to the kitchen. What was up there?

She put a foot on the first rung.

Would you want him in your room, prowling around your things? her conscience chided.

She couldn't force herself to take another step. She went back to the rocking chair and picked up her sewing, but the ladder kept beckoning her.

The rug slid off her lap, and she marched with determination back to the ladder. That time she made it to the fourth rung before she backed down again.

"I'm either going up or going out," she said.

Then you'd better put your coat on. You can live with going out. You can't with being nosy.

She checked on the chicken again, grabbed her cape from a hook beside the back door, slung it over her shoulders, and opened the door. Bitter cold air hit her in the face, but she didn't care. She knew how a bird felt when it was finally let loose from its cage.

She flipped her hood up and set a course for the barn. A few white wispy clouds drifted around in the sky, but the sun was shining even if the wind was biting. She ducked inside the barn and went straight back to the stalls. Her horse hung his head over the gate, and she rubbed his ears.

"You thought I'd forsaken you, didn't you? I bet you haven't even been exercised, have you? What kind of plantation is this that doesn't even have enough men to ride you? Well, we can sure fix that in a hurry, can't we?"

She went to the tack room and located a bridle, put it on the horse, and led him out into the middle of the barn. Then she set about saddling him up for a ride. No one was around, so it didn't matter that she was wearing a dress. Her cape would cover any bare skin if the dress flapped up.

The saddle was heavier than she remembered, and she was huffing by the time she got it cinched. The first time she attempted to throw her leg over the saddle, her foot got tangled up in her dress, and she almost fell flat on her back before she righted herself. The second time, she hitched her skirt up to her waist and had no problems at all. She tucked the cape in to keep modest and rode out of the barn.

The big black beast was hard to hold back. He'd been in jail too many days, and he wanted to run, but she didn't know her way around the farm, so she kept him at a steady trot. Isaac had said that his and Micah's house was on the far edge of the property, but was it the western edge or the east? If she rode to the north, would she be on Burnet property still, or would some farmer think she was trespassing and shoot her?

She reined in the horse and let him prance around the house twice before she saw the trail leading off toward a wooded area. That was the way Micah had driven when he took Mama Glory away. She held the horse to a trot and guided him down the path. Two wagon ruts with brown winter grass between them testified to the fact that people came and went that way fairly often.

A squirrel barked at her when she entered the pecan grove, and a possum lumbered across the road in front of her. She'd ridden half an hour when a wild turkey flew up and spooked the horse. Holding on when he reared wasn't easy, but she managed to get him under control.

"It was just a big old overgrown chicken!" she said breathlessly, when she could catch her breath. She turned the horse around and let him have his head, running full out toward the cabin. If she burned the dinner, Isaac would know that she'd been out of the house. If he told Micah, then Mama Glory would find out, and Fairlee would never get to go to Delia's.

Isaac watched the men plowing from the corner of the field. Ben had everything in control, but Isaac liked to keep in touch with his overseer on a daily basis. Two teams of mules pulled the heavy plows over the rich black earth, getting it ready for spring planting.

He hooked a leg over the saddle horn and thought about Fairlee. She was getting stronger every day. The way she stared out the window said that she was about to go plumb stir-crazy. He remembered when he'd known the same feeling in the San Antonio jail. He would have fought Santa Anna with nothing but a butter knife to get out of that place. Fairlee wasn't going to stay penned up in the cabin for a whole month. She might not go to Delia's, but she was about to bust out, and he wasn't sure what to do when she did.

"How are things up at the cabin with your woman?" Micah asked.

Isaac jumped. "Where did you come from?"

"Been sitting here for a whole minute. Your mind was a million miles away," his brother said. Micah was a year younger than Isaac, had brown hair that he parted on one side, eyes the color of pecan shells, and was twenty pounds heavier.

"I was thinking about that jail," Isaac said.

"Outlaws and angels, huh, brother?" Micah chuckled.

"Only we weren't really outlaws, and those Lavalle women dang sure weren't angels."

"No, but Tyrell still thinks he got an angel, so we won't say that too loudly." Micah laughed again.

"If he did, he got the only angel in the bunch."

"Which brings us back to my question. How are things up at the cabin with your woman?"

Isaac bristled. "She's not *my* woman. Why did Mama Glory leave her up there without a maid or a woman in the place? I'm surprised that Delia lets it go on. If it gets out that Fairlee's been up there with just me for a whole month, she'll be a marked woman. We'll have to whup every man in the state for saying bad things about her."

"You could always make an honest woman of her, and that would stop any wagging tongues," Micah suggested.

"Why don't *you* make an honest woman of her?" Isaac challenged him.

"Not me, man. I've got a woman. You know me and Sally Duval been seein' each other all winter. I think it might be serious," Micah said.

"You love her?" Isaac asked.

"Not like Tyrell does Delia, but I'm not sure that kind of love is for me. I don't know that I could give my whole heart away like he did. How about you?"

"It'll be all or nothing with me," Isaac said.

"Which is it with Fairlee?"

"I have no idea. That woman makes me so mad, I could eat nails one minute, and the very next I want to protect her. I don't want to leave her alone, and yet we do have some big arguments. Kind of reminds me of the times when Momma and Daddy used to disagree. Maybe I've been around her too long. Does Sally have a sister?"

"No, just Sally. If we three hadn't had to go on that wild goose chase to Texas, she and I might already be married. We were getting pretty serious last year, but by the time we got back, she was interested in Lewis Johnson, and I backed off."

"Lewis married Edna Overland in the fall. What happened there, do you reckon?" Isaac asked.

Micah shrugged. "Guess Edna made him feel all warm and gushy."

Isaac slapped at his brother with his hat. "Does Sally make you feel like that?"

"Nope, but she'll make a good wife."

"Father didn't think so," Isaac said softly.

"I know he didn't. I never did figure out why. He said he'd tell me when he came home from his trip up to the cabin. He wanted to think things through before he said too much, and then he was dead," Micah said.

Isaac frowned. "He went up there to think about Sally Duval?"

"I always figured it was just an excuse to go remember Mother. Maybe he thought Sally wasn't enough like her and needed to figure out what Momma thought. You know he used to say that when he went up to the cabin, he could almost hear her talking to him."

Isaac nodded. "It looks like Ben's got things under control. I'm going back to the cabin. Fairlee is making dumplings. Want to join us?"

Micah shook his head. "No, sir. Mama Glory would have my hide tacked to the smokehouse door. She says nobody is to go near that cabin until she says so."

"Ever wonder how she got so much power?" Isaac smiled.

"Because Mother gave it to her. We didn't

have grandparents around, and Mama Glory helped raise us. I'm not crossing her, not even for chicken and dumplings. It'll all be over in a couple more weeks, brother. I miss you at home."

Isaac nodded and rode off toward the wooded area between him and the cabin. He'd just cleared the woods when a motion up ahead caught his eye. He'd recognize that cape anywhere, and that big black horse. He reined up and watched Fairlee ride like a bat set loose from fiery hell.

Fairlee slid off the horse the minute she was in the barn, tied the reins to a stall gate, and tore across the lawn as if the devil was licking at her skirt. She threw open the kitchen door and raced to the stove, where the chicken had all but boiled dry. She added a teakettle of water to the pot and sat down to catch her breath.

"That was close," she said.

The front door blew open, and Isaac stood there with his arms folded across his chest. "Where have you been, and why did you leave your horse sweating in this kind of weather without rubbing him down?"

She glared at him. "It's not dinnertime. What are you doing home?"

"It's close enough. Now answer me."

She stood up so fast that the chair flipped over with a loud bang. She stormed across the floor until she was inches from his nose. "Don't you talk to me like that. I'm not a child. I don't have to answer to you, and where I've been is my business. I didn't infect anyone, so you can come down off your high horse."

He leaned forward into those flashing blue eyes — and kissed her. Like the time before, it just happened, as if he had no control. Their kiss had the intensity of a tornado, complete with flashing lightning and rolling thunder. His head reeled, and he wanted more.

Fairlee put her hands up to his chest with the intention of pushing him away, but she couldn't. Kissing Isaac was even more exhilarating than the cold wind in her face as she'd raced home to check on the dinner.

When he broke away and quickly turned his back, she said, "I'm going out to take care of my horse. Did you rub yours down before you came in here acting like a dictator?"

Apparently, the kiss didn't affect her the way it did him, or she wouldn't be able to speak a word. He shook his head.

"Then I guess we've both got something

to do before dinner, don't we?" She stormed out the kitchen door, leaving him alone to wonder if all their kisses would be as shocking and passionate.

CHAPTER TWELVE

Fairlee mumbled and muttered the entire time she made dinner. She'd come back inside loaded for bear, but Isaac wasn't there. She didn't owe him an explanation, but she hadn't ridden back to the house in a hurry because she was afraid he'd catch her outside. The chicken was what had set a fire under her horse's hooves. She didn't want to burn the bird after she'd gone to the trouble to wring its neck, heat the water to scald it, and then pluck all the feathers that morning.

She poured milk into the flour, added the rest of the ingredients, and dropped the dumplings by teaspoons into the boiling broth. While they steamed, she removed the chicken meat from the bones and added it back to the mixture. She sliced half a loaf of bread, set the table, and poured coffee into two mugs. She got out butter and plum jam and poured salt into two crystal salt wells.

"Might be doing every bit of this for nothing. He may have lit a shuck for home and didn't even look back. He's afraid of an argument that he knows he'll lose," she said.

Isaac yelled down from the loft. "Who are you talking to?"

She jumped and tried to remember everything she'd said in her rambling anger.

"Your dinner is ready, and your horse is taken care of as well as mine," she told him.

He climbed down the ladder. "I had planned on riding him again after we ate, so it wasn't necessary. What were you fussin' about anyway?"

"That is my business and none of yours," she told him. "What were you doing up there in the middle of the day anyway?"

He sat down at the end of the table. She grabbed the heavy pot from the top of the stove, wrapped a towel around the bail, and carried it to the table. "You didn't answer me."

Isaac filled his plate. Truth was, he'd gone to the loft to think. He'd watched her stomp all the way to the barn, throwing her arms around as if she were telling Tempest or Delia a story. He'd planned on slipping down and going out the front door when she returned. That way he could circle around the house and go to the barn while she finished preparing the meal. But he could see through the big doors, and he'd watched her take care of her horse, then unsaddle his and rub him down. The whole time her lips moved furiously, as if she was arguing with an invisible demon. He was almost glad he couldn't hear her while she worked her way through that.

"I was thinking," he said. That wasn't a lie. He had been going over and over the two kisses they'd shared and trying to convince himself that they were nothing but byproducts of too much time together.

"What were you thinking about? No, don't tell me. I'll tell *you* something *I've* been thinking about. I'm not staying cooped up in this cabin every day anymore. I might not be able to go to Delia's yet because of the fever, and I will keep up my end of the work, but I'm going outside every day, and if you don't like it, you go home, and I'll stay here for the rest of the month by myself. I'm going to ride my horse when I'm danged good and ready. He needs exercise, and you can't stop me." She sucked up another lungful of air to go on with her tirade.

He pointed his fork at her. "It wouldn't do me any good to gripe at you anyway, because you are a Lavalle, and you'll do exactly what you want, no matter if it kills off the whole plantation. So ride your horse when you are danged good and ready, and drop dead if it kills you, being out in the air so soon after the fever."

She slapped at the fork. "Just so long as we understand each other."

Tension was so thick that sweet words couldn't have melted it. But neither Fairlee nor Isaac had any sweet words to say anyway. They were battling their own feelings as they came to realize that they were attracted to each other, and they feared that if they were sweet even for a minute, they'd lose not only the battle but the war.

Fairlee vowed that she would fight the attraction and would never succumb to it. It was far too soon after her ordeal over Matthew for her to trust another man, much less an outlaw. Simply being thrown together with Isaac the past month had brought on the foolish notion that she liked him.

She stole a glance across the table at his dark, brooding face. Isaac truly was an onion. The first layer was handsome, but once she started peeling away, she found more and more things to like about him. He was kind and considerate. He didn't have to do what Delia had asked him to do. Fairlee wouldn't have done it. Not even for

Delia. The Burnet brothers had been eager to get away from the Oak View plantation, even happier to leave Tempie and Fairlee behind. To travel all that distance again with the promise that he'd bring Fairlee back to Delia meant he was a good man.

Or a dumb one, she argued.

Isaac felt her stare and ignored it. He'd been a fool from the get-go to let Delia talk him into such folly. Fairlee was a beautiful woman but far too spirited for him. Tyrell had the energy to live with a Lavalle on a daily basis. A month had taught Isaac that he wasn't that big of a man. Sure, their two kisses had turned his heart into a quivering mass inside his chest. But surely there were other women in the area who could create the same emotions. He might be ready to take a wife, but Fairlee wasn't the right one for him. He'd be glad when the month was up so that they could part company and he could begin to look for someone like Sally Duval. A woman who'd be willing to let the man in the family wear the britches — quite literally.

"What are you doing this afternoon?" she asked coldly.

"I'm going out to help Micah. We're having the fields plowed for spring planting, and if it gets cold enough tomorrow, we're going to butcher and smoke a couple of hogs," he answered flatly.

"So you've been seeing your brother every day? You could have brought me news of Delia."

"She's fine."

"That's all? Just 'fine'?" Fairlee barked.

"Don't jump all over me just because I didn't think to bring you news every day of your sisters."

"Sisters?" Fairlee asked through gritted teeth.

"Tempest got here a couple of days ago. Your Uncle Jonathan sent an escort. She brought two covered wagons full of things. Stuff from Oak View and your things as well as hers. Tyrell said he'd have to build another house to take care of all you Lavalle women. I told him to build you your own house or make you stay in the barn. Ain't no house would hold three of you," Isaac said.

"You talked to Tyrell too? I suppose you've seen Delia?"

Isaac shrugged. "Most every day."

Fairlee pushed her chair back with such force that it landed on the floor with a thud. "Every day!" she squealed.

"You've got to stop throwing furniture around. You'll break the chairs," he said.

"To the devil with the furniture. I'll buy a new chair if I damage this one. Did Delia and Tempie even ask about me?" she asked.

His brow drew down as if he were thinking hard. "They said for me to keep you out here until you'd cooled down. Tempie said it might be best that you stay until after the baby comes, so Delia won't be upset."

"You are a pig from Hades," she said, and she stormed off to her room. She slammed the door with such force that it rattled the lamp on the mantel. Isaac's laughter didn't do a thing to dampen the heat of her mad spell.

"You are an angel from up above, walkin' on clouds and singin' sweet songs," he yelled through the door.

She opened it to find him right in her face. "Don't you be sarcastic to me."

He leaned in and kissed her soundly, then turned and strolled out of the house.

She slapped a hand over her mouth to see if it was as hot as it felt and was surprised to find cool lips. How could they feel so normal when every nerve in her body was on fire?

Isaac saddled his horse and rode back toward the wooded area. That third kiss was even more powerful than the first two. In a natural fire, such heat would burn itself out in a matter of minutes. They could never live together. In a year's time they'd either be dead or wish they were and miserable for the rest of their lives.

Matthew Cheval didn't know what a lucky fool he was. The next time he went looking for a woman with money, he'd do well to make sure she didn't have a drop of Lavalle blood in her.

Like the dutiful little wife she wasn't and would never be, Fairlee set her kitchen chair upright and cleaned the dishes. Then she donned her coat and went to the barn, where she worked in the tack room all afternoon. By the time she was ready to head inside to make supper, she left behind a space that was organized and spick-and-span; even the floor had been swept.

So tired that she had trouble picking up her feet, she trudged back to the cabin, only to have the mournful spiritual hymn, "Roll, Jordon, Roll," meet her when she opened the kitchen door. Warmth, accompanied by baking sweet potatoes and frying ham, rushed out to wrap around her like a warm blanket.

"Mama Glory?" she yelled.

"I'm in here makin' your supper. I come to take you home. Woman that can spend all afternoon out there in the barn is well enough to go on home. We'll be leavin' right after you and Mister Isaac eat. He don't know it yet, but I reckon he'll be mighty glad to get you delivered, so he can get on about his work. I heard tell that Sally Duval has set her sights on Mister Micah and that Mister Isaac is askin' around if she's got a sister or a cousin. Looks like them boys is all going to wind up married in a year of each other. Come on in and shut the door. Wind's cold you're letting in."

Fairlee eased the door shut, removed her coat, and hung it on the hook beside the door. Her heart fell into her boots and refused to beat. Suddenly she wanted a few more days to think about what Isaac's kisses might mean. She wanted it all settled before she went to Delia's.

Mama Glory was staring at her. "That make you happy?"

"Of course it does. I'm going to be so glad to see my sisters. Do you know what they did to me on the day before my wedding?"

Mama nodded slowly. "They saved your life. That man was pure poison. Miz Delia was worried nigh out of her mind about you. I was afraid she'd worry herself so much, she'd lose that baby. If you've a mind to go over there and fight with her, then I won't let you go. You promise me right now you'll be glad to see her, or I'll tie you to that bed in there and keep you here until after the baby comes."

"I promise. I'd never do anything to hurt her or the baby. I'm so homesick to see them both that I don't even think I can fight with them," she whispered.

"You better keep that promise, or you'll be sufferin' the wrath of Mama Glory, and it's worse than God's wrath. He'll forgive a sinner. I won't."

Isaac dreaded going back inside. Fairlee had had all afternoon to fret and gather ammunition for another big fight. He'd far rather kiss her again and see if it lit up the cabin and sent another dash of whiskey-type warmth through his veins. He removed the saddle from his horse and carried it to a spotlessly clean tack room.

"I guess I know what she's been up to all afternoon. Maybe she's worked out her anger and frustration and will be civil. Maybe I'll read another story, and we'll talk again."

He had a spry step in his walk across the backyard, but when he noticed the wagon on the north side of the cabin, his feet were suddenly too heavy to take another step. That was Tyrell's wagon, and there was only one reason it would be there.

"Well, come on in here and shut the door. We got supper ready for you to eat, and then we're all goin' home. The wagon is out there all ready for us to be gone. I done took care of gettin' things ready to go. Ain't no use in leavin' behind good food, so we'll take it all back with us. Don't reckon anyone will be comin' back out here for a spell unless Micah decides to marry up with Sally Duval and bring her here for a little honeymoonin' time." Mama Glory talked nonstop while she put the food onto the table.

Isaac looked at Fairlee.

She raised one shoulder in half a shrug.

"You got your speech all ready?" he asked.

Mama Glory stopped what she was doing and crossed her arms over her expansive chest. "Ain't goin' to be no speech. Not one thing is going to happen to make Miz Delia worry or be sad. This is a happy day. Three sisters is goin' to be together once and for all, and there won't be a mean word said, will there, Miz Fairlee?"

"No, ma'am."

"Huh!" Isaac snorted.

"What's that all about?" Fairlee snapped at him.

"I'll believe it when I see it," Isaac said.

CHAPTER THIRTEEN

The ride took the better part of an hour. Both horses had been tied to the back of the wagon, and Fairlee sat beside Isaac, with Mama Glory riding in the rear, bundled up with a quilt around her shoulders and hair. She chattered the whole way about how happy Miz Delia was going to be to see her sister home at last.

Home! Fairlee didn't feel like she was going home at all. Home was Oak View in Louisiana. That's where she'd been born and raised. Her father, Captain Lavalle, had brought his bride there, and they'd had the three girls in between the endless times he was off to some godforsaken part of the countryside with the military. Uncle Jonathan and Aunt Rachel were fine surrogate grandparents, and Fanny and the nannies were always around to help. And when Captain Lavalle did come home for a month or two, everything was better than wonder-ful.

But *home* as Delia and Tyrell Fannin's house? Fairlee didn't think so.

Isaac drove the wagon past a large white house with four big porch pillars holding up a balcony for the second floor. "That's where I live," he said.

"Nice." Fairlee nodded.

Mama Glory smiled.

They rode another quarter of an hour, and Isaac pulled up reins in front of another big house with a wide veranda that looked newer than the rest of the house.

"This is it," Isaac said.

Mama Glory was out of the wagon before either one of them could help her. "Manny, you get up off that porch and get on out here and help tote this stuff to the kitchen."

"Yes, ma'am. I been sittin' here waitin' on you. Miz Delia said y'all would get here soon," the teenage girl said.

Mama Glory ambled off. "I'm goin' on to make sure the kitchen is in good shape. If it ain't, I reckon I'll be lookin' for another girl to come to the house and help me."

Manny picked up two full feed sacks and followed Mama Glory inside. "It's so clean, you could eat off the floors."

"Then I expect you did a fine job while I

was gone," Mama Glory said.

Isaac hopped down from the wagon seat and went to help Fairlee down. He put his hands around her small waist and lifted her to the ground, wishing the whole time that he had the right to pull her to him in a final hug or maybe even a brief kiss. But before he could do either, Delia and Tempest threw open the double doors and rushed outside.

Tempie moved faster than Delia and reached Fairlee first. She threw her arms around her in a fierce embrace, tears rolling down her cheeks. "Please tell me I'm forgiven."

"And me too." Delia joined them in a three-way hug.

Fairlee's blue eyes misted, and she wiped at them with the back of one hand. "Of course you're forgiven. I've missed you both so much, I couldn't possibly be mad at you. Let's go inside, and you can tell me everything that has happened in the last month. Don't leave out anything. Did you have any trouble getting here, Tempie? Did you bring all our things? What about you, Delia? Is the baby all right? You don't think I'll give you the fever, do you?" Fairlee talked fast and wiped away another tear. She could never be mad at her sisters for longer than a day, and she could've danced a jig right there because they were all together again.

"Thanks for bringing her home," Delia said, as Isaac took his place back on the wagon seat and snapped the reins.

"You're welcome. My job is done. I'm going home for the night soon as I get this wagon unhitched and put Fairlee's horse in the stables," Isaac said.

"We're having a celebration tomorrow night. You and Micah will come, won't you?"

Isaac nodded. "If Micah doesn't have something planned."

Delia smiled. "Tell him to bring Sally. I'd love to meet her. And even if he does have something else planned, we'll look for you. We'll be seeing both of you anyway tomorrow at the butchering. Come on over here and have breakfast with Tyrell. Mama Glory will fix enough for an army. Y'all might as well eat here before you get started."

"We'll see. Good night, ladies," Isaac said.

Delia hooked her arm through Fairlee's and led her into the house. "You've got to talk first before we tell anything. Isaac told us about those men in the stage telling you what happened with Matthew. That rat! I could strangle him with my bare hands."

The doors opened into a wide foyer, with a credenza with a gold mirror above it on one side and stairs on the other. An open doorway on the left led to Tyrell's office. He waved at them to come inside and met them halfway across the room.

He hugged Fairlee and then wrapped an arm around Delia. "Hello, Fairlee. We're glad you're well enough to come home. Did the trip tire you?"

"I was fine a week ago. I'm glad I didn't have to stay away the whole month," she said.

"Mama Glory knows best about fevers. She says some women would take even longer than a month but that you're tough," Tempie said.

"Come on into the parlor, and Manny will bring in some hot tea to take the chill off," Delia said.

Fairlee felt as if she and her sisters were walking in a dream instead of reality. Not one thing was right. She almost wished she'd stayed in the cabin, because absolutely nothing was familiar. Not the house. Not her sisters. Even in their joy at being together, something was different.

She was sincerely glad for the first time that she hadn't married Matthew if this was what marriage brought about. She let Delia lead her to the parlor and sat down in the wing chair she was taken to. Tempie spread a quilt over her legs, and then she and Delia sat on each end of the matching settee.

Fairlee threw the quilt off. "I'm not sick anymore. I'm fine, and I'm not cold, and I spent the whole afternoon cleaning out the tack room in the stables, so I'm not an invalid. Mama Glory said I couldn't fight with you two, but she didn't say I had to play like I was half dead."

Tempie giggled.

Delia laughed out loud.

Fairlee glared at both of them.

"Our sister is finally home," Delia said.

"I believe she is. Do you have any idea how worried we've been about you?" Tempie asked.

"You should have worried about Isaac. I came close to shooting him at least a dozen times." Fairlee finally smiled.

"Ah, and we thought you two might fall in love," Tempie teased.

"After Matthew, I've decided to be an old maid," Fairlee said. "You can have Isaac, Tempie."

Tempie pointed at her own chest. "Me! No, thank you. I'd rather cut off my hair and join the military as a man."

Fairlee laughed so hard at the vision of that that she had to wipe her eyes. "That's probably what we both need to do. The world would be a safer place."

Tempie's eyes glittered with mischief. "But not until Delia has the baby, right?"

"Baby, my eye! Delia isn't having a baby. That's a whole litter," Fairlee said.

Delia threw a pillow at her at the same time that Manny opened the door and carried in a silver tray with a teapot and three cups on it. She stopped dead just inside the door and stood perfectly still.

"Mama Glory is going to have a fit," she whispered.

"We aren't fighting. We're just teasing," Fairlee told her.

Manny grinned. She was a tall, thin girl with beautiful brown eyes and a long, narrow face. When she smiled, her whole face lit up. "She's been fussin' that your Fairlee might cause a stir in here."

"Not me. I'm the angel child. These two are wolves in sheeps' skins," Fairlee protested with a grin.

"Oh, yeah, as if any of us could ever be an angel. Only time we came close was when we were dressed up as nuns," Tempie said.

Manny set the tray down and crossed herself. "Mister Isaac told Mama Glory you were all a handful."

"Oh, he did, did he?" Delia poured the tea.

Manny nodded.

"Well, we are," Tempie confirmed.

"And we don't intend to change," Fairlee said.

"My, oh, my!" Manny shook her head as she went back to the kitchen.

"So?" Tempie looked at Fairlee.

"What?"

"We want to know the details. All we've gotten out of Isaac is that you caught a fever before he could get you home. What all happened? Was it as exciting as the trip from Texas?"

"Was yours?" Fairlee asked Tempie.

"No, it was as boring as listening to Uncle Jonathan read a chapter from Job on Sunday morning when we were little kids. But I was traveling in a wagon for two weeks. You were kidnapped. Was it thrilling?" Tempie answered.

"It was a nightmare. I understand why you did it, but did you have to do it that way? Couldn't you have let him take me to our cousins' for a visit?" Fairlee sipped the tea that Delia handed her.

Tempie shook her head. "You were being too mule-headed for that. We had to get you as far from Matthew as possible, and Delia wanted us both to be here with her, so that seemed the best way to do it. Did you sleep a long time? I got worried I'd given you too much of Uncle Jonathan's medicine."

Fairlee looked at them over the top of her teacup. "How would you like to wake up in the hull of a boat with thunder and lightning all around and a snoring man in the corner?"

Delia set her teacup down. "I told you she'd make a good story out of it. I swear, I'm not going to bed until I've heard every detail. So start talking."

Fairlee got to the part where she woke up to find Mama Glory in the cabin before she stopped. The clock in the foyer chimed ten times, and Tyrell poked his head in through the parlor doorway.

"Delia, darlin', you should be in bed. Fairlee is going to be here a long time. You can talk tomorrow."

"He's right," Fairlee said. "Go on up to bed, and we'll finish this tale tomorrow."

Delia set her jaw in an expression Fairlee had seen often. "But I want to hear it all. I've been waiting and worrying, and now that you're here . . ."

Fairlee stood up and held out a hand to Delia. "And I'm not going anywhere, so we'll finish tomorrow. Truth is, I do not want the wrath of Mama Glory to fall on my head if you take sick because of lack of rest. She assures me it's worse than the wrath of God."

Delia took her hand and hauled her rounded body up from the settee. "Believe me, it is. She's worse than Fanny."

Tempie looped an arm through Fairlee's. "I wouldn't cross her. Come on, I'll show you your room. We already unpacked your things. Won't you be glad to see your own clothes?"

Fairlee looked down at the outdated dress she wore. She hadn't thought about her own things in a very long time. "Yes, it will. Did you bring me more trousers? Mama Glory cut mine up for a rag rug."

Tempie's eyes popped wide open. "She didn't!"

Fairlee nodded emphatically. "Yes, she did."

"Well, we'd best hide our pants, then," Tempie said.

"Hide what?" Tyrell carried a lamp in from the study.

"You take Delia on up. We'll follow behind," Tempie said.

Tyrell kissed his wife on the cheek and hugged her to his side with his free hand. "With pleasure. Are you glad to have them both under the same roof with you again, darlin'?"

"More than you'll ever know," Delia said.

Tempie stopped at the first room to the left off the landing and opened the door. Lamps had been lit, giving the room a soft golden glow. Fairlee's nightclothes were laid out on the bed, and a sweet-looking servant sat in a straight-backed chair, waiting to see what she could do to help.

"This is Dotty. We'll share her," Tempie said.

"Pleased to meet you, Miz Fairlee. Mama Glory has told me all about you. Would you like a full bath? There's water already warmed for your washin' up if not. Can I help you out of that dress?" Dotty asked.

"No, you go on and take care of Tempie. I can do for myself tonight, since you've brought up hot water. Thank you, Dotty."

Dotty curtsied and turned to Tempie.

"Another cup of tea would be nice before I go to bed."

"Yes, ma'am." Dotty disappeared into the dark hall.

Tempie touched Fairlee's arm. "Are you really okay?"

Fairlee patted her sister's hand. "Yes, I am. I was well days ago. I could have come home the day I woke from the fever."

Tempie pulled her sister over to the bed and made her sit down. "I'm not talking about fever. Did you . . . when you . . . when

246

those men talked so mean . . ."

Fairlee giggled. "I'm a Lavalle. I may be the only Lavalle in history who got hoodwinked by a money-grubbing rogue. But you and Delia took care of me. Just rest assured, I may do the same to you if it looks like you're about to make a similar mistake."

"I won't," Tempie said seriously.

"Never say never. Now, you'd best go on to bed. I understand we're butchering tomorrow," Fairlee said.

"Bet you wanted to do some butchering during your trip, huh?" Tempie started out of the room.

"Yep, but not hogs or steers." Fairlee laughed. "Good night, Tempie."

"Good night, Fairlee. I'm glad we're all under one roof again."

"Me too." She made her way across the floor to the washstand, stripped down to bare skin, and washed away the dust and grime from the day. Then she slipped her nightgown over her head and ran her hands down the front of it. It was her gown, her brush and comb set on the vanity, her hairpins in the small crystal container, her dresses in the wardrobe, and her trousers in a drawer.

She let her hair loose and brushed it, counting each stroke until she reached a hundred. Each time the brush went from her scalp to the end of her long black tresses, she wondered what Isaac was doing at that moment. Was he already snoring, or was he so glad to be among his own personal effects that he couldn't sleep?

She laid the brush on the vanity and crawled beneath the sheets. The feather bed caressed her like a mother holding a child. She remembered Isaac's kisses and touched her lips. When she went to sleep, she dreamed about Isaac Burnet.

Isaac paced the floor in his bedroom. It was warm, the bed had been turned down, he'd had a long, soaking, hot bath, and the tub had been taken away, and he'd tried everything from reading to staring at the glowing embers in the fireplace. Nothing worked.

His mind ran in circles. Was Fairlee doing all right with her sisters? She was sure to explode if she didn't speak her mind, and if she did explode, Delia might have that baby too early.

He looked out the window toward the other house, but there was no way he could see it. He smiled when he figured out that things must have been settled peacefully, because there was no yellow glow where Fairlee had gone up in flames and set the whole place on fire.

Finally, he stretched out beneath the covers on the feather bed and sank down into the softness. He laced his fingers behind his head and stared out the window at the shadows created by the moonlight drifting past the tree limbs and into his room. Was Fairlee having trouble adjusting to her old, familiar lifestyle? Did she miss the simplicity of the cabin? Or the excitement of the journey?

His eyelids finally grew heavy, and he slept, only to dream of Fairlee the way he did most nights anyway.

Chapter Fourteen

Everything was in a bustle in the kitchen the next day. The men doing the butchering brought meat into the house to be ground and seasoned for sausage, packed into white muslin tubes, and taken back out to the smokehouse to be hung from nails. Hams had to be rubbed with Mama Glory's special mixture of sugar cure before being hung in the smoke from smoldering hickory chips.

Fairlee and her sisters were everywhere at once. It wasn't their first butchering day, and they knew how to issue orders as well as take them. Delia was allowed in the kitchen but only to supervise, and she had to do it from a rocking chair drawn up close to the cookstove.

While she seasoned and chopped, Fairlee looked for Isaac but only caught a glimpse of him once all day, when he carried in a pan of pork chops that Mama Glory had requested for supper that night. He hurried right back outside and didn't even glance her way.

"Hey, did you hear that we're invited to Sally Duval's tomorrow evening for dinner?" Tempie asked Fairlee.

Delia groaned. "I can't go."

"Of course you ain't goin' to no dinner five miles away. You're goin' to stay right here until that baby comes. You ought to already be restin' in bed while you wait for the baby," Mama Glory told her, ferociously rubbing a ham.

"Not me. Mother said that just made a woman weak. I'll go to bed when the baby comes, and I'll only stay there a couple of days," Delia told her.

"You'll stay ten days and not a day less. Woman's insides go back together on the tenth day," Mama Glory said.

"We'll see." Delia smiled at Fairlee. Delia was the tallest of the three sisters and had the straightest black hair and the lightest eyes. Aunt Rachel had thought it odd that each daughter had gotten progressively shorter, their eyes darker, and their hair curlier. She often said she'd have liked to see the fourth girl. She'd have been under five feet, had hair so kinky a comb wouldn't go through it, and navy blue eyes.

As if reading her mind, Tempie said, "Hey, you reckon if this is a girl, she'll have kinky hair and dark blue eyes?"

"I've decided that she's going to look like Mother," Delia announced.

"Have you decided on names?" Fairlee asked.

"Something simple, like Jane," Delia answered.

"No Fairlee or Tempest?" Tempie teased.

Delia shook her head. "Nope. The simpler, the better."

"Okay, tell me about this dinner party. Why are we invited anyway?" Fairlee asked, crumbling some sage into a meat mixture.

"I guess Sally wants to show Micah that she can be sweet and lovable to his shirttail kin," Tempie said. "Besides, she's got a cousin staying with her for a month, and she wants Isaac to meet her."

A hot jolt of pure green jealousy ripped through Fairlee's veins. "Trying to do some matchmaking, is she?"

"Might as well. A man gets to his age, it's time," Mama Glory said. "It's way past time for you two girls to be thinkin' about a husband. When the baby comes, we'll be havin' some parties to make you known to the men around here. I'll see to it that you each find a good husband."

Fairlee almost dropped the sage. "Don't be looking on my account. I'm never going to marry."

Mama Glory laughed so hard that tears rolled down her cheeks. "I reckon you'll live to eat them words."

"She's a prophet," Delia said from her corner.

"Maybe so, but not where I'm concerned. Can I wear my trousers and boots and ride over on my new horse?" Fairlee asked Tempie with a wink.

Mama Glory threw up her hands. "You still got any of them abominable things, you best keep them out of my sight, or I'll make more rug rags out of them."

"Well, I suppose if we're going to be allowed to leave the house, we'd best be dressed properly. Your midnight blue velvet might be nice, Fairlee. I'll wear the red watered silk. How's that?" Tempie said.

"And you'll ride in a closed carriage with Washington in the driver's seat. I don't like that Sally Duval, but there ain't much an old woman like me can do when a man gets his mind set," Mama Glory muttered.

The hair on Fairlee's arms stood up. "Why don't you like her?"

Delia replied first. "She says something wasn't right the first time Sally and Micah were flirting, back before they chased the killer to Texas. Mama Glory knows things."

Mama Glory narrowed her eyes and nodded slowly. "Yes, I do. I feel things in my bones, and I see and hear other things. People talk in front of me because they think us servants don't know nothin'. Something ain't right, and I just know it. Micah is about to get into more trouble than you did, Miz Fairlee. Y'all keep your eyes and ears open over there and see what you think. I ain't trustin' that cousin of hers none either with Mister Isaac. Tomcats ain't got a lick of sense when a girl cat goes to flickin' her tail in his face. Men ain't no better."

Delia started giggling, and the mirth spread to Fairlee and Tempie.

Micah slipped in the back door and stared at all three of them. "What is so funny?" He remembered the first days on the trail from San Antonio, when he'd still thought the sisters were nuns. Even then they got tickled at the strangest things.

"Mama Glory was telling us about tomcats," Delia said.

Micah looked at Tempest. "What about them?"

"What women discuss in the kitchen ain't a bit of your business," she told him without blinking.

"Did you tell Fairlee about our dinner invitation?" he asked.

"I did, and we will be there on time. Fairlee wanted to know if we could ride over on our horses and wear our trousers. We could entertain the guests with stories of our trip," Tempie said.

Micah rolled his eyes toward the ceiling. "Don't you dare."

"I bet he doesn't want us to pick our noses or put part of our supper in our pockets for later either." Fairlee joined in the teasing.

Micah left without a word and slammed the kitchen door behind him.

"You girls are goin' to drive them two brothers mad before the year is out," Mama Glory said, chuckling.

"And you love it, don't you?" Delia asked.

Mama Glory nodded. "You just watch that Sally, and I'll be waitin' for you to tell me what you think."

"You trust our judgment?" Tempie asked.

"If you got the sense your sister has, then you'll do fine to spy for me."

Fairlee couldn't control the giddiness she felt as she dressed for the dinner party. She pulled her wavy hair up into a twist and let Dotty help her into the blue dress with the wide tucked collar strewn with pearls. Matching pearl buttons went from the nape of her neck to the hem of the dress, and she fidgeted while Dotty deftly fastened them all. She hadn't been to a dinner party where she got all dressed up since before her mother died.

"Don't be nervous. You're prettier than that Sally Duval woman," Dotty said.

"Have you seen her cousin?"

"No, ma'am, I ain't seen her, but I bet you're prettier than her too."

Tempie sashayed into the room, her red satin dress rustling as she walked across the floor. "My, but you do look pretty all cleaned up. Isaac might even throw the cousin out in the yard in the cold for you."

"And is Micah going to throw Sally out for you?" Fairlee shot back at her.

"I'm not interested in Micah Burnet."

Fairlee looked at her reflection in the mirror above the vanity one more time. "What makes you think I'm interested in Isaac?"

"I'm only teasing. He's going for an introduction to Sally's cousin. He had his chance with you. Besides, I can't see anyone with your fire and determination married to someone as dark and serious as old Isaac Burnet," Tempie said.

"He's not old. He's only twenty-three, and

that's just three years older than I am. And yes, he has dark hair and dark green eyes, but he's not all that serious. Actually, we had a few good laughs after he abducted me." Fairlee picked up a short velvet cape and flipped it over her shoulders.

"Washington should be bringing the carriage around front about now," Tempie said. "I forgot to tell you, but we're all riding together. No sense in taking two carriages. Washington can take all four of us."

"And when did you intend to tell me?" Fairlee asked.

Tempest stepped behind her. "Right now. Go on down there and let Isaac see what he lost."

Isaac looked up from the bottom of the stairs, and his breath caught in his chest. Fairlee was beautiful in her trousers and boots; she was lovely in her calico dresses; but the vision in blue floating down the stairs came close to convincing him that she was indeed an angel.

Micah had the same reaction when he glanced up and noticed Tempest in her deep red satin. He was glad that he had an interest in Sally, because the feelings that shot through him when he looked at Tempest could destroy him. He should never live with a woman with that much power over him. He had every intention of asking Sally to marry him within the next couple of months, and that should end the way Tempest Lavalle affected him when he looked at her.

"You are two lovely ladies this evening. I'm sure Sally will be glad to make your acquaintance. Washington has the carriage ready out front. May we escort you?" Micah held out his arm for Tempest.

Isaac did the same and got ready for the tingle down his spine when Fairlee looped her arm through his. He was not disappointed.

"Tell me about Sally," Fairlee said, when they were inside the comfortable carriage with their feet on warmed bricks wrapped in flannel.

"She's the niece of our neighboring plantation owner, Vincent Duval. Her father and mother were both taken with a fever two years ago, and her uncle took her into his home. He and his wife have two sons who are grown and married with children of their own," Micah said.

"And will those sons be there tonight?" Fairlee asked.

Jealousy filled Isaac's soul. "Why do you ask?"

"Just wondering who all we might meet."

"No, one lives in Jackson and is a lawyer there. The other is in Washington, D.C., and works for the government. Neither will be there. Sally says the guest list includes her and her cousin and two cotton buyers from back east who are staying with her uncle while they work on a deal."

"Ten of us, then?" Tempest asked.

Micah nodded. He avoided looking at her even in the semi-darkness of the carriage. She was beautiful, but she was also a force of nature. When she was around him, it was as if all the air was sucked from his lungs, and he couldn't breathe. She probably affected all men that way, whether they were married or not.

"Nice-sized dinner party. What about the two cotton buyers? Do we have names?" Fairlee asked.

Micah nodded. "Evan Smith and Joseph Wilson. And Sally's cousin is Constance Duval. She is Vincent's brother's daughter. That brother lives in Jackson," Micah said.

"Evan, Joseph, Constance, Sally, and what is Vincent's wife's name?" Fairlee asked.

"Edith," Isaac said.

"A perfect party. Five women and five men. That should give you two plenty of opportunity to do some serious flirting,"

Tempest said.

Her tone was so brittle that Fairlee spun around to see why her sister's voice had changed. Tempie's chin was tilted up, and she looked down her nose at Micah. It was the first time that Fairlee realized Tempest had feelings for Micah Burnet. What a tangle! She couldn't wait for the evening to end so she could quiz her sister.

The carriage stopped in front of a stone mansion that rose up three stories out of well-groomed shrubs and trees. Fairlee could visualize it in the spring and summer with the roses in bloom and the yard a splash of color from the flower beds. The depth of the porch, its roof supported by a dozen enormous white pillars, would provide welcome shade in the summertime sun.

Washington hopped down and opened the carriage door for them. They were met at the double doors by the butler before they even knocked. He took their coats and wraps and motioned for them to join the rest of the party in the parlor.

For a split second Fairlee wanted to bolt and run. She didn't want to meet Sally or her cousin, nor the senior Duvals or their cotton-buying friends. She wanted to go back to the cabin up in the woods and become a crazy old hermit woman who raised cats and roses.

Sally crossed the room and said, "How delightful to see you." She talked to all four of them but kept her eyes trained on Micah.

Fairlee watched Tempest, whose bright smile didn't reach her eyes.

"You must be the Lavalle sisters. We've heard so many things about you. I'm Sally. This is my cousin, Constance, my Uncle Vincent and Aunt Edith, and our guests, Mr. Smith and Mr. Wilson from New York."

Micah made introductions. "And this is my brother, Isaac, whom most of you already know, and my cousin's sisters-in-law, Tempest Lavalle and Fairlee Lavalle."

Sally had brown hair and big doelike eyes. Her face was long and narrow and her lips thin. She was taller than either Fairlee or Tempest. Her gold-colored velvet dinner gown was nipped in at a small waist, and her bosom rose and fell rapidly when she looked at Micah.

Constance was definitely Sally's cousin. Her hair color was the same, as were her brown eyes. Her face was rounder, but her lips were just as stingy. She was the same height as Sally. Her dress that evening was the same color, only it was satin instead of velvet, and it had rosettes at the bosom.

Aunt Edith was as round as she was tall

and a perfect match for Uncle Vincent, who was built the same way. Both of the cotton buyers were in their mid to late fifties and bald, with chubby faces reminiscent of babies.

"We are honored to have you in our home," Edith said. "Would you like a cup of hot tea while we wait for dinner to be served?"

"No, thank you," Tempest said.

"Maybe a glass of water," Fairlee requested. Watching Constance size up Isaac so blatantly made her mouth dry.

Instantly Edith went to the side bar in the parlor and poured a crystal glass half full. She handed it to Fairlee with a smile. "You girls have such unusual names."

"Our mother named all of us for angels," Fairlee said.

Isaac covered his mouth quickly when he coughed.

Fairlee gave him the meanest look she could conjure up on short notice.

"Of course, our names are all that is divine, I'm afraid, because our father taught us to ride and shoot and take care of ourselves like boys," Fairlee went on.

"Oh, dear!" Constance fluttered her hand in front of her face. "I can't imagine doing such things. Do you really shoot a real gun?"

Fairlee tipped up the water and drank it all, then set the glass back on the sideboard. "Yes, as well as a bow and arrow. And we all three handle a knife fairly well too."

"Well, bully for your father," Evan Smith said. "I had a tutor teach my two daughters the same things. They might need to know how to defend themselves someday."

"Thank you for understanding," Fairlee said.

Tempest found a tapestry-covered wing chair and slid down into it. Sally wasn't anything like she'd pictured. She could at least have had a wart on her nose or a high, squeaky voice, but she didn't. She was really quite attractive in a boyish way.

"Do you really do those things too?" Sally asked.

Tempest looked up. "Guilty as charged. It's a good thing we knew how to take care of ourselves when we made the trip from Texas to Louisiana with these outlaws," she added.

That brought on a whole raft of questions. By the time the girls had answered a dozen of them, it was time for dinner. Micah offered Sally his arm, and they followed Vincent and Edith into the dining room. Evan was quick to offer his arm to Tempest and to tell her on the way that she reminded him of his daughter back in New York. Joseph Wilson escorted Fairlee, leaving Constance and Isaac to bring up the rear.

The dining room was aglow with three candelabra set at perfectly spaced intervals down the table. Bowls of pumpkin soup sent spirals of steam toward the twelve-foot-high embossed ceilings. Place cards were set beside the soup bowls, and servants waited in the background for their jobs to begin.

Vincent sat at the head of the massive table with Edith to his right. Isaac was seated to her right with Constance beside him. Evan sat beside Constance. Micah had the honored position at the end of the table with Sally to his right. Joseph, Fairlee, and Tempest were lined up on his other side.

Fairlee almost laughed at the arrangement. She would have at least put Joseph between her and Tempie. It was a direct slap from Sally, showing them that they were only there to even out the numbers for a good dinner party. Micah had a place of honor and was as far removed from either Lavalle as she could get him. Constance was beside Isaac so that there could possibly be a touching of hands when they reached for something.

"How delightful. I love pumpkin soup. Our cook, Fanny, makes it for us at Oak

View," Fairlee said.

"Oak View. Over in western Louisiana, right?" Evan asked. "We're sending some contacts that way this spring to talk to Mr. Lavalle about buying his cotton."

"Well, ask Fanny to make you some pumpkin soup. I'm sure you'll enjoy her cooking," Fairlee told him.

The soup was followed by an entrée of pork roast, mashed sweet potatoes, green beans, and hot rolls. When Vincent had polished off his plate, servants came out of the woodwork to efficiently remove the dishes and replace them with saucers holding chocolate pie.

"My favorite," Micah said.

"I know," Sally murmured.

Tempie stiffened beside Fairlee. Yes, ma'am, they were going to have a long, long talk before they went to sleep that night. They might even wake Delia and get her two cents' worth on the issue.

A foot kicked Fairlee's toe, and she immediately looked at Tempest, but she had her head down, working on the pie. She looked to her left, and Joseph was motioning for his wineglass to be refilled. Across the table Isaac looked miserable and nodded toward the door.

She smiled.

They'd both rather be outside in the cold carriage than sitting at the table with these people. They'd traveled with each other enough that they didn't even need words to relay messages anymore.

Constance touched his arm. "Tell me about this trip you've just returned from. Do you often go that far?"

He shook his head. "Delia wanted her sisters to come and be with her. So I was sent to bring Fairlee."

"Not Tempest?"

"No, she came along later. I fetched just Fairlee." He blushed.

"Well, I smell a story. We'll have to work up a picnic for Micah, Sally, you, and me as soon as the weather is nice. I'd love to hear all about it," Constance said.

No, you wouldn't, and if you did, you sure wouldn't have me sitting at your cousin's table again, Fairlee thought.

"Not much to tell. It was a long, boring ride," he said.

Fairlee kicked him in the shin.

He clamped his jaw shut to keep from yelling.

Constance pressed on. "Oh, you didn't bring servants and wagons?"

"No, it was just the two of us," Fairlee interjected. "I was in a bit of a hurry to get here, since my sister wanted one or both of us with her when the baby comes. So Isaac was good enough to provide an escort. And he is so right. It was a very long and boring ride. We were able to use the stagecoaches until we got to Monroe, but then it was horseback and sleeping wherever we could find a roof," Fairlee said.

"Your father did teach you right," Evan said.

Constance threw a hand over her mouth. "How horrible! I can't imagine that kind of thing. My father would never let me travel like that. Didn't you think of your reputation?"

Couple of times, ma'am. Let me tell you about the nights we slept in the same hotel room. Or how about the time we each took a bath in the room with the other one sitting not five feet away in a rocking chair? Fairlee thought.

"My reputation was as good as gold in the hands of a Burnet man. They are perfect gentlemen in every sense of the word," Fairlee said.

"See? I told you Micah was a gentleman." Sally all but swooned when she looked at him.

"Well, let's have our after-dinner brandy in my study, gentlemen, and leave these women to talk about the finer things in life," Vincent said.

"I'll see you later," Sally whispered to Micah.

He smiled, but it did not reach his eyes, Fairlee noticed.

The men followed Vincent out of the dining room.

Edith stood up. "Ladies, shall we take our after-dinner tea in the parlor, where it's more comfortable?"

They followed her like dutiful little schoolgirls into the parlor, where she sat in a wing chair like a queen. Servants brought tea in a silver pot along with the daintiest of floral china cups arranged around it.

"Sally, darlin', would you pour for us?" Edith asked.

"I'd be delighted," she purred.

Fairlee watched her closely. She had to report to Mama Glory, and so far there had been nothing of note that she could put her finger on. Of course, the fact that Tempest was attracted to Micah didn't help her make an impartial judgment. If Tempest wanted the man, then Fairlee would just naturally find everything wrong with Sally.

"So, tell us about where you grew up. Oak View, was it?" Edith asked.

"My father and his brother owned the

place jointly. My father was a military man — he lost his life at the Alamo in Texas last spring. Mother had died of a fever the winter before. He was always being sent off to one post or another, so we stayed at Oak View with Aunt Rachel and Uncle Jonathan," Fairlee said.

"And now you'll be living with Delia and Tyrell?"

"Yes, ma'am," Tempest said.

Edith set her teacup down and clapped her hands. "You'll be delightful guests for dinner and parties. I'm planning a spring masquerade that will last a week. You will have to come."

"Thank you," Tempest said, without committing her or Fairlee to attending.

"And now you were going to tell us about the trip that brought you here so quickly," Constance said.

Before Fairlee could say a word, Isaac poked his head into the doorway. "Ladies, I hate to rush you, but we must be going. Are you ready?"

Fairlee could have kissed him smack on the lips for interfering. "Yes, we are. Please rest assured, the story is as boring as the trip was," she said to Constance as she set her cup down and prepared to leave. "Thank you for a delightful evening, Miz

Edith. We'll have to arrange something at Delia's after the baby comes and return the favor."

Edith walked with them to the door. "That would be very nice."

Sally caught Micah's eye and smiled at him. "Perhaps you'll ride over later in the week?"

"Perhaps," he said, as he put on his coat and hat.

"Good night, then," Isaac called over his shoulder as he ushered Fairlee and Tempest out the door.

Washington opened the carriage for them, and in minutes they were inside, the Burnet brothers on one side and the Lavalle sisters on the other.

"Did you see how well we Burnet boys behaved? And you thought we weren't anything but ragtag outlaws," Micah said.

"Well, you thought we were nuns and, later, worse than sinners," Tempest told him.

"And you didn't even think we'd be presentable for your dinner party that night," Micah continued. He wanted a rousing good argument with Tempest. He wanted to latch on to something that he couldn't stand about the woman.

"You didn't think we were presentable in our trousers and boots, did you?" Tempest

270

reminded him.

"Truce," Isaac said. "You two stop arguing. We all had a fine time. The food was good, though I really did not like that pumpkin soup. I'd much rather have plain old potato soup."

"So, what did you think of Constance?" Micah asked Isaac. "Sally was eager to know, but I couldn't very well ask you in front of her."

Isaac was miserable. He could lie about pumpkin soup and make himself eat it to be a gentleman. Lying about a woman was a very different thing.

"I think she liked you very much," Tempest said.

Fairlee could have strangled her until she turned blue.

"I'll save my judgment until I know her better. I only met the woman tonight. First impressions aren't always right," Isaac said.

Fairlee didn't know she was holding her breath until she let it all out in a whoosh, then covered it up by pretending to yawn. "They were both lovely ladies. A little prim and proper for our taste, but that's what appeals to men, isn't it, Tempie?"

"Oh, yes. According to Aunt Rachel it is," she agreed.

They fell silent then, each in his or her

own thoughts the rest of the way to the Fannin house, where Isaac walked the two women to the door. "Good night, ladies," he said.

"Good night," they chorused.

"And now the talking begins," Fairlee said, when they were inside the door and on the way up the stairs.

"Yes, it does. You like Isaac," Tempest said.

"And you like Micah," Fairlee told her.

"Yes, I do like him, but it won't do me a bit of good. Besides, he's bullheaded, so I shouldn't like him. But I do, and it's plain as day that Sally doesn't really like him, let alone love him. She looks at him the way Matthew did you. She's seeking to be the mistress of a plantation, and she'll do anything to get that. She's poor as a church mouse and wants to be rich," Tempest said.

"Is that what you're going to tell Mama Glory?"

Tempest threw herself into a chair in Fairlee's room. "Dotty, darling, would you go to the kitchen and get a platter of whatever you can find? And three cups of the hottest, blackest coffee. We girls are going to be up for a long time."

"Three?" Dotty asked.

"Delia will be here in a minute."

"Oh, I see," Dotty said.

"Did I hear my name?" Delia's stomach preceded her through the doorway. Her white muslin dressing gown had an enormous collar and billowing sleeves caught at the wrists with cinched cuffs.

"You did. Micah is about to make a mistake. We may have to send someone to kidnap him if Tyrell can't talk sense into the man," Tempest said.

"What's your opinion, Fairlee?" Delia motioned Tempest from the rocking chair and eased down into it.

"She doesn't have one. She was too busy trying to keep from slapping that silly Constance. She's got her eyes on Isaac. I think they're in cahoots and want to live together over at the Burnet place," Tempest said.

"Fairlee?"

"I'm going to tell Mama Glory that I need more time to form an opinion about Sally but that Constance is definitely ready to lead Isaac to the altar," Fairlee said grimly.

Fairlee had barely gotten into bed and tucked the covers up around her neck when something rattled against her window. She figured a bird had been drawn to the flicker of the fire and was trying to get inside, but then she remembered that birds went to roost when the sun went down.

The next racket brought her up out of bed to ease her curiosity. She pulled back the heavy winter drapes to see the figure of a man standing below her window. Just as she looked down, he slung a handful of pebbles against the glass. When he saw her in the window, he motioned for her to come down to the yard.

She looked at the clock on her dresser. It was well past midnight. Another glance out the window as the moon came out from behind the clouds revealed that her pebble-thrower was Isaac Burnet.

She slipped on a dressing gown and hurried down the stairs. Something must have happened to Micah for him to be out at such an hour, but he didn't want to disturb Delia. She threw open the door, and he rushed inside.

"Is Micah hurt?" she gasped.

"No, why would you ask about Micah?"

"If he's not hurt or sick, then why are you here?" she asked.

Suddenly Isaac felt really silly. It had seemed so right when they'd gotten home, but now, with her right there before him, it was obviously absurd. What could Fairlee Lavalle see in him? She could have any man in the whole state.

"I can't do it," he said.

"Do what?" She tapped her foot.

"I can't pretend to like Constance."

"Then don't. No one says you have to like her. Just be honest with her, the way you are with me," she said.

"I'm not . . ." He hesitated as he tried to form the words.

"You're not what?"

"It's different with you."

"Why? Because I'm Delia's sister, and we've been through two hellacious trips together? I'm just a woman. I'm not an angel."

"I felt like Constance was looking at me the way Matthew did you that night we had supper at Oak View. Like she doesn't even see me. You don't look at me like that," he said.

"No, I don't, but then, I'm not interested in your money," she said.

"What would you do if you were in my shoes?"

"What would you do if you were talking to me instead of Constance?" Fairlee asked.

"I'd tell you to set your sights on another man and get the devil out of Mississippi." He laughed at his own audacity.

She giggled in turn. "Then that's what you tell her. Except you don't actually say it.

275

You just stay the devil off their plantation and lay low for a few weeks until she sets her sights on another man."

"You make me laugh," he said.

Her heart soared as high as the moon and stars. She didn't have to worry about Constance! Now, if only she could make Micah see the light.

"Okay, then, I'm going on home," Isaac said.

"Good night," Fairlee told him.

He took a step forward and gathered her into a fierce embrace. She looked up when he relaxed his grip and barely had time to close her eyes before his lips touched hers. The moon and stars floated down from the sky and danced around them. She heard the prettiest fiddle music in the distance, and her heart wouldn't stop racing.

"What was that all about?" she asked.

"Thank you for the advice and for being you." He let her go, stepped out the door, jumped onto his horse, and rode away.

She stood there speechless and watched until she couldn't see him or even hear his horse's hooves beating on the ground anymore. Was this what it was like to really be in love? She'd have to talk to Delia about it the next morning.

She eased the front door closed and went

up to her bedroom. Dropping her robe on the back of a rocking chair, she sighed loudly and then crawled in between the sheets. The ceiling became a canvas painted in turn by every memory she'd ever shared with Isaac. There he was that first morning when he'd thought she was a nun. Next came all the times they rode side by side from Texas to Mississippi. Then the morning he'd left Oak View with his brother and cousin. She'd never told Delia how jealous she was when Tyrell came back for her. She finally shut her eyes and tried to sleep, but she couldn't. The kiss they'd just shared had fired up her senses, making slumber an impossibility.

Isaac rode like a madman for the better part of a mile, and then he drew the reins up and stopped the poor horse dead still. He was in love with Fairlee Lavalle. Just when it had happened, he had no idea. But he was, and he couldn't go home until he told her. He turned the horse around and slowly headed back.

When he arrived in the yard, he sat there for a very long time, trying to get up the courage to throw a handful of gravel at her window again. How did he tell her, and what if she laughed in his face? It had only been a few weeks since she'd been stung by that rascal Cheval. Should he wait and court her?

He wrestled with the idea and finally decided that they had spent more time together than any two people who courted for a whole year. If he courted her, he'd see her maybe three hours a week. They'd just spent a whole month together, twenty-four hours a day, seven days a week. If he did the arithmetic, he was sure that would come to a year or more of courting.

Finally he picked up a handful of pebbles and threw them at her window.

At the rattling at her windowpane, Fairlee opened the curtains and looked out, not a bit surprised to see Isaac there again. If that kiss had set his mind to reeling the way it had hers, then he probably had something to say, and she dang sure had things she wanted to say to him. One being that she didn't want him to see any other woman.

"Okay, Momma, I know a lady doesn't tell a man such a thing, that it's forward and out of place, but ladies don't wear trousers or ride astride a horse either. So I'm a different kind of woman," she whispered all the way down the stairs.

She opened the front door and walked

into his open arms.

Isaac tilted Fairlee's chin up and kissed her again. It was exactly like the others; it came dang near to knocking him to his knees and caused his ears to ring.

"I'm just me, Fairlee. I didn't mean to do it, but I did, and now I have to tell you, or I can't live with myself. I'm miserable, and the only way to ease it is to speak my mind."

She hoped she knew what Isaac was going to say before he uttered a word, but if she'd had to speak or be shot at daybreak, she would have put on the blindfold and stood against the wall.

"I don't even know when it happened. Looking back, I think it was on the way from Texas, even when you were a nun. I knew it wasn't right, and I fought it, and then you weren't a nun, and it still didn't seem right. But that's when it started, and I've been battling with my heart and soul for a year, and I'm tired of the fight," he said.

She took a step forward. "Would you please kiss me again and shut up?"

The kiss was gentle at first, but then it deepened into something that let out all the pent-up passion in his soul.

She laid her head on his chest and listened

to his racing heart. "Me too, Isaac. I don't know when it happened either, but I realized it tonight when Constance was flirting with you. I hated it, and I wanted to throw my pumpkin soup at her."

"I love you, Fairlee Lavalle. I have for a long time, and I'm admitting it right now. Will you marry me?" Isaac asked.

The stars blurred, and the moon jiggled. "What did you say?"

Isaac tipped her chin up for another kiss. "I asked you to marry me. I know we'll fight, but Tyrell assures me that the making up is worth it."

"I love you, Isaac, and yes, I will marry you, and yes, we will fight, but you were wrong about one thing."

"Here we go," he said.

"I wasn't walkin' on clouds with Matthew. But I am now."

A week later Fairlee Lavalle and Isaac Burnet were married in the living room of the Fannin house. Mama Glory was in her . . . well, her glory. She made a huge white cake with sugar icing and insisted that Fairlee wear Isaac's mother's wedding dress, a frothy lace garment that they had retrieved from the attic.

Fairlee made a trip through the kitchen

on her way to the parlor to let Mama Glory see her in all her wedding finery. "What do you think?"

"I think I was right the first time I saw you layin' in that bed with the fever. That man was in love with you even then. It just took you two stubborn souls a while to figure it all out," Mama Glory said, as she put the final touches on the cake. "That's why I made you stay out there with him. To give you time to figure things out. You could've come home two days after the fever broke."

Fairlee stuck a finger into the icing bowl. "Then why did you bring me back before the month was out?"

"You needed to be together, and then you needed to be apart, to see if you could live with each other and then without each other. Don't you get that sticky stuff on your dress, girl. Get on in there. The clock just rang ten times. Mister Isaac is a nervous wreck for fear you'll change your mind."

Fairlee licked her finger. "I won't ever change my mind."

"Then go and say the words so he'll quit his frettin'."

Fairlee hugged Mama Glory and kissed her on the cheek. "You are wonderful," she said.

"Not me. I'm just a meddlin' old woman who sees things other people is blind to," she said, but she was still smiling when Fairlee slipped out the door.

Fairlee picked up a bouquet of pansies from the foyer and met Isaac in front of the hearth.

"You sure are handsome today," she said, as she looped her arm through his.

"And you are beautiful," he said.

Delia smiled.

Tempest giggled.

Tyrell and Micah grinned.

"Dearly beloved," the preacher began.

In ten minutes they were legally married, and Isaac kissed Fairlee soundly before them all, making her his bride.

"I love you," she whispered when he broke the kiss. "And, darlin', I'll be walkin' on clouds until my dyin' day."